AMERICAN RONIN

PHILIP CAINE

AMERICAN RONIN

First paperback edition printed 2017 in the United Kingdom

ISBN 9780993374845

Published by REDOAK
www.philipcaine.com
For more copies of this book, please use the website above.

Critique & Editing: Gillian Ogilvie
Technical Editor: Malcolm Caine

Cover Design: www.gonzodesign.co.uk

Printed in Great Britain by:
www.print2demand.co.uk

ABOUT THE AUTHOR

Philip's career began in hotel management and then transitioned to offshore North Sea, where he worked the boom years on Oil Rigs, Barges & Platforms. Seventeen years passed and Philip returned to onshore projects taking a three year contract to manage accommodation bases in North & West Africa.

From Africa, Philip moved to the 'Former Soviet Union' where he directed multiple projects in Kazakhstan & Russia, a particularly exciting seven years where dealings with the KGB were an everyday event.

The end of the Iraq War in 2003 took Philip to Baghdad where, as Operations Director, he controlled the operations & management of multiple accommodation bases for the American Coalition. He left Baghdad in 2010.

The last three years of his career were spent running a couple of support services companies in Iraq, with head offices in Dubai.

Philip's time in the Middle East has been the inspiration for his adventure thrillers, and the JACK CASTLE series.

Philip semi-retired in 2014 and began writing fiction in February 2015, after joining Ulverston Writers Group. His first novel, PICNIC IN IRAQ, is an adventure treasure hunt set in Iraq. The sequel, TO CATCH A FOX, is an exciting rescue mission set in Syria. BREAKFAST IN BEIRUT, sees the main character, Jack Castle, working for MI6 in the Middle East. His fourth novel, THE HOLLOW PRESIDENT, reveals the truth about a corrupt and murderous American President.

AMERICAN RONIN is his fifth book in the JACK CASTLE series.

Also by Philip Caine

'The Jack Castle Series'

PICNIC IN IRAQ

TO CATCH A FOX

BREAKFAST IN BEIRUT

THE HOLLOW PRESIDENT

In 12th century Japan the Shoguns, or Warlords, ruled.
The law was based on the Bushido code, in which honor
and loyalty were paramount.
The noble Samurai were the defenders of the law and
gave fealty to their Shogun masters.
But there were Samurai who had fallen from grace,
Samurai who held no respect or loyalty for anyone,
Samurai who sold their swords to the highest bidder.
These disgraced
Samurai, were known as, RONIN . . .

AMERICAN RONIN
Prologue
Autumn 2008

The floor was cold beneath his bare feet and the air-conditioning made his naked body shiver slightly. The other two men in the room looked on disinterested as a third snapped away with a large camera.

'Turn around,' said the cameraman.

He did as instructed and listened to the click of the shutter as the photographer took more pictures of his body.

'Okay, that's it. You can get dressed.'

On the table was a small pile of new clothes, under-shorts, cotton slacks, a T-shirt and a pair of light canvas shoes. The photographer checked the camera, nodded to the other men and left the room.

'Move your ass, 716,' said the bigger of the two men.

'Where am I going?'

'Just get dressed.'

He looked at the big man as he pulled on the slacks. 'Taking pictures of me to show I have no cuts, bruises or scars. You're taking me back to the States.'

The shorter of the two spoke. 'Just get dressed, you fucking traitor.'

After putting on the T-shirt he smirked, then held out his hands.

'That's right, 716,' said the big man, as he clipped on the handcuffs, 'you're going back.'

716 continued to smirk, as a cloth hood was pulled over his head.

The heat hit him the moment they left the building but the fresh air in his lungs was a blessing. He didn't know where he'd been held for the last four months, but he knew it wasn't America; definitely a CIA black-site, probably somewhere in South America, somewhere out with the old US-of-A; a place where they could interrogate anyone without any regards for their human rights, a location they could deny all knowledge of, if it ever came to a Congressional enquiry. He could hear the familiar sound of a chopper engine, as the two men walked him towards the aircraft.

'Step up, 716.' It was the big man's voice.

He stumbled as he climbed in. He took his seat and felt the belt being clipped around his waist. The engine noise increased and the helicopter shook as the rotors gathered speed. Within a few seconds they were airborne. The fresh air blowing in through the open doors was cooling and pleasant. *Back to America*, he thought as he closed his eyes and slipped into a half sleep.

He didn't know how long they'd been flying, maybe twenty or thirty minutes, but the sound of the alarms and the voice of the pilot shook him wide awake.

'What the hell's going on?' he shouted.

No one answered. He could hear the pilot yelling, 'MAYDAY! MAYDAY!' as the helicopter began to spiral out of control, nose-diving towards the ground a thousand feet below. The last thing 716 heard was the big man's voice screaming, 'Oh, my God!'

Three days later he woke to the sound of birds chirping and the rays from a warm morning sun coming in through the open door. He tried to move but a woman's voice said. 'Be still, señor.'

Her body blocked the sun's rays as she stood next to his bed. She knelt beside him and supported his head, a small cup of water to his mouth. 'Drink. Slowly.'

Through cracked lips he sipped the cool liquid and then laid his head back on the thin pillow. He couldn't see her face as it was in shadow. 'Where am I? Who are you?'

'You are at my grandfather's farm, señor, and I am Consuela, Consuela Sanchez.'

'What the hell happened?'

'You were in helicopter, señor. It crashes.'

He frowned, the pain in his head building. 'Yes . . . yes, I remember. What about the other men?'

'I'm sorry, señor. The others are all dead.'

He sucked in a deep breath and felt the pain in his chest. 'How'd I get here?'

'My grandfather found you. He was out on the hills with the goats and saw the helicopter fall.'

'How long have I been here, Consuela?'

'More than three days.'

He tried to move, but the pain in his head was increasing. He looked down and saw his torso was heavily bandaged and his leg strapped into a crude splint.

He groaned. 'How badly am I hurt?'

'Your leg is broken and three maybe four ribs also. You have bad head injury and I think your nose is broken. My grandfather and I bind your ribs and make the leg straight. I put the stiches into your head, but we do not know how to fix nose. Sorry, señor.'

The pain in his head was bad now, but he managed a weak smile. 'Sorry? You saved my life. You fixed me up pretty good. No need for sorry, Consuela.'

She moved to the other side of the bed and checked the splinted leg. He turned his head and looked at her face as the sun shone through the door. She was young, maybe nineteen or twenty, with long dark hair dark and huge eyes, in a kind face. She smiled and said, 'You must rest now. No more talk. My grandfather will be home soon.'

'Where is he?'

'He has gone to Isthmus, señor.'

'Isthmus? Isthmus de Panama?'

She looked puzzled. 'Si, señor.'

'I'm in Panama?'

'Si, Panama. And what is your name, señor?'

He looked up into the big brown eyes. '716.'

'Señor?'

He grinned slightly and said, 'My name is Greg. Greg Stoneham.'

Chapter One
Summer 2009
'Gregory, Greg to his Friends'

It was a couple of minutes before midday on the outskirts of Istanbul. Greg Stoneham's eyes narrowed as he watched the feedback on two laptops, each of which displayed the view from the cameras on two separate drones, one in Washington and one London. The simultaneous feedback made him smile, as the two tiny aircraft flew unchallenged towards their respective targets.

In London, Big Ben began to chime eleven o'clock. Six rotors buzzed loudly as the fast moving drone increased speed and came in low over Vauxhall Bridge. Across the river on the roof of the Tate Britain Museum, the young drone pilot expertly controlled the agile machine. The small control panel's display showed the same view as the monitors in Istanbul. At the north end of the bridge the drone increased altitude slightly and then veered to the left, towards the SIS building, the home of the British Secret Service.

The pilot touched the ARMED icon on his remote control and watched as the swift aircraft shot towards the iconic building. His concentration was shattered as the roof-access door behind him burst open. A dozen heavily armed security officers flooded onto the roof, their automatic weapons blasting away, killed him instantly.

The sound of the drone was lost in the gunfire, but not so the explosion. On impact, the tiny aircraft decimated the Patio Restaurant, killing and injuring over forty security service personnel.

The Washington laptop showed the view from a camera slung beneath the drone. At five o'clock in the morning there were not many vehicles on the Georgetown Pike. The sidewalks were almost deserted, with only a few city cleaners going about their daily routine. The removal van parked at the side of the road did not attract any attention, even from the police car as it drove slowly past. In the back of the truck the drone pilot flew his remote aircraft expertly along the wide boulevard towards the huge CIA complex at Langley. At one hundred yards from the main building the aircraft gained altitude and veered off to the right and out over Langley Ford Park, then continued to climb into the early morning sky.

The back of the van was stuffy and hot. The pilot was sweating heavily as he concentrated on the small monitor. He touched the ARMED icon, then brought his drone back in a wide arc towards the headquarters of the CIA. In the centre of the complex the outdoor restaurant was serving breakfast to over a hundred security personnel and admin staff. The sudden appearance and high pitched buzz of the swift moving aircraft became the focus of their attention.

In the back of the van, saline sweat stung the pilot's eyes and he blinked repeatedly to clear his vision, then expertly flew the drone into the centre of the crowded restaurant.

Stoneham looked at his watch and continued to smile, his mind racing at the success of the mission, *both attacks carried out almost simultaneously, great planning, great execution. Fucking CIA what did they know? They hadn't a clue what was going on half the time and the goddam Brits were just as bad. MI6, another joke.*

He closed down the laptops and placed them carefully into the aluminium briefcase. He looked around the room and was satisfied nothing remained of his presence here these last two days. He went to the window and checked the side street. Nothing out of the ordinary, a few locals going about their business, some kids playing, and the occasional vehicle. He opened the door slightly and checked the corridor. No one. Casually he left the room, purposely leaving the door unlocked. With luck some squatter or hooker might take up residence, thus totally destroying any possible trace evidence of his being there.

Gregory, Greg to his friends, Stoneham, was in his early fifties, born in a small backwater town in Louisiana, the only son to a storekeeper father and music teacher mother. After college he had joined the Marines, where he served with distinction, eventually operating in military intelligence. His abilities had not gone unnoticed and when he left the service at the age of forty, he was quickly recruited by the CIA.

His years in the Middle and Far East, as well as time in the Former Soviet Union, began to jade his opinion of the CIA and how it operated, and in 2006, while running a black-ops team in Afghanistan, he was approached by an Al Qaeda intermediary. From that moment forward he'd worked as a double agent and been paid handsomely into his Montenegro bank account.

It wasn't until he became involved in an operation with a bunch of British ex-professionals that things went wrong for Greg Stoneham. The Brits were to go into Syria and rescue their buddy Jack Castle and, while doing so, capture Professor Hassan Al Hamady, the second in command of ISIL, code named The Fox.

The mission had gone well, right up until the time the Blackhawk, with The Fox on board, was shot down. Stoneham, monitoring the operation from the American base at Erbil in Kurdistan, heard the Brits had captured masses of intelligence and fearing his involvement with the terrorists may be exposed, aborted the extraction of the British team, leaving them to fight their way out of Syria alone.

What Greg hadn't bargained for was the determination of this guy Jack Castle to seek revenge for abandoning him and his men in Syria. Castle and his buddy Tom Hillman had tracked Stoneham to a five star hotel on the Asian side of the Bosphorus. Surprisingly Castle and Hillman had not killed him, electing instead to hand him over to the boys from Langley. The subsequent months were spent enduring relentless and often painful interrogation, at the hands of the CIA, in the Panamanian black-site.

But fate had intervened and, as a result of a fortuitous helicopter crash while being transferred back to the States, Stoneham had escaped. His feelings of hatred for the security service he'd once been so loyal to had now become all-consuming. Now, his sole purpose in life was to inflict as much harm as possible to the CIA, MI6, and if possible, Jack Castle.

Chapter Two
Spring 2012
'The Library'

The Topkapi Library does not live up to its elegant name, as it is more of a large reading room than a library. Located on the Asian side of the Bosphorus, in the suburbs of Istanbul, it is hardly ever frequented by anyone other than the locals in the area. Smelling of cigarette smoke and fusty books, and with worn and shabby furniture, it is decidedly unwelcoming but, for Greg Stoneham, this was an ideal place for a secure initial meeting.

After waiting for over an hour, he was irritated and annoyed. He was about to leave, when he felt a gentle tap on his shoulder. With a slight start he turned and looked at the woman standing behind him. 'Good morning, Mr Stoneham.'

She moved round and took a seat on the other side of the small table. He stared for a moment, surprised at the appearance of the expensively dressed woman in front of him. She looked Eurasian, maybe thirty five or six, slim, with a strikingly beautiful face, long black hair tied back in a thick ponytail and eyes that sparkled in the poorly lit room.

'You're late. And don't use my name,' he said.

She sensed his annoyance, but smiled and said, 'Thank you for meeting me. Actually I've been here for almost twenty minutes. I was watching you from the other side of the library. I wanted to ensure all was safe before we met.'

The comment did nothing to ease his irritation, and he said curtly, 'Of course it's safe. Otherwise I wouldn't have said to meet here.'

She leaned across the table and fiddled with the newspapers. 'Of course, of course,' she said, the smile ever present, 'You know your business, Greg. May I call you, Greg?'

'Sure, just keep your voice down.' Stoneham looked around the tired old Turkish establishment; no one was paying them any attention. 'You certainly match the description I was given, but I have to say you don't look anything like I expected.'

'Should I take that as a compliment?'

'Take it any way you like, honey. But where I come from you would certainly be considered a good looking woman.'

She frowned; clearly not interested in the westerner's predilection for the way a woman looked.

Stoneham smiled. 'Like I said, you match the description, but I still need t'see the photograph.'

She took out her smartphone and swiped the screen, then handed it across the table. Stoneham nodded at the picture displayed, a shot of the Statue of Liberty, the very same he'd sent to his contact several days earlier, to be used as confirmation of ID at this meeting. 'Okay, good. So who're you, honey?'

The frown returned for a second and then she smiled. 'I am Hana Chang and I am a colonel in the North Korean Ministry of State Security. Please call me Hana.'

'Okay, so what's the deal, honey, sorry, Hana?' He leaned forward and said quietly, 'What do the North Koreans want with me?'

She didn't speak for several seconds, as she took-in the man before her. He was totally bald with a vivid scar above his right ear, thin, but not emaciated and certainly fit looking for a man in his fifties. Next to his chair was a fine walking cane with an ornate wolf's head chased in silver. The most distinctive feature was his broken nose, which could have looked almost comical, if it were not for the emotionless eyes above it, dark, almost lifeless eyes that never stopped moving, taking in everything, yet giving away nothing.

'We have a proposition for you, Greg. Your reputation precedes you and we feel you are just the person to work with us on this project.'

It was Stoneham's turn to frown. 'Really? And what project might this be?'

'I am not at liberty to discuss that at this stage. My instructions are to escort you from Istanbul to Pyongyang, where you will be fully briefed on what we require from you. What I can tell you now is, your bank account has already been credited with fifty thousand dollars for taking this meeting. You may leave now and no more will be said and you will never be contacted by us again. No hard feelings, as you say in America.'

The frown on Stoneham's face eased. 'And if I don't leave?'

'Then you will travel with me to Pyongyang, where you will be offered twenty million dollars to direct the project.'

Surprised he said, 'Twenty million? So not just a hit on some poor bastard in your government then?'

Chang's smile faded slightly. 'We are not in the habit of killing our ministers Mr Stoneham.'

'No, of course you're not. And I said, don't use my name. Go on.'

Her smile re-appeared. 'As I was saying. The project will be outlined and you will be expected to accept the contract. Once you are aware of what we require, there will be no turning back.'

Stoneham's eyes narrowed, his thoughts of what a twenty million dollar contract would mean to him . 'And if I decide to walk away?'

She looked around the library, quietly cleared her throat and continued. 'You will not be allowed to walk away, Greg. You will not leave Pyongyang alive.'

He grinned and sat back in the big old armchair. 'So, it's an all or nothing deal?'

'Indeed so. All or nothing. You have fifty thousand today. You could have twenty million tomorrow.'

He smiled and leaned forward, offering his hand. 'In that case, you gotta deal, lady.'

Chapter Three
'A Gilded Cage'

The flight from Istanbul's Ataturk Airport had been extremely comfortable in the executive jet. Hana Chang had cleared Stoneham's departure using pre-prepared diplomatic papers, so there was, to all intents and purposes, no record of the American leaving the country, never mind travelling on a North Korean aircraft. The plane had landed in the early hours of the morning and Stoneham, still escorted by Hana, was driven to the outskirts of the city. He was not surprised when they arrived at a military installation. Although Spartan on the outside, the accommodation he was given was quite luxurious.

'It's almost four o'clock,' said Chang, as she showed the American around the suite of rooms. 'I'll be back to pick you up at ten in the morning. Everything you need is here and there is plenty of food and drink in the kitchen. I must apologise for the security, but this place is, as I'm sure you will agree, quite comfortable. There will be guards outside, which again I'm sure you will understand the need for.' She nodded to a telephone on the table. 'That will get you straight through to me should you require anything.'

He grinned. 'Yeah, sure. A gilded cage. It's fine.'

'Then I shall bid you good night, or should I say good morning, Greg.'

After she left the room, Stoneham went into the kitchen and took an American beer from the refrigerator. He smiled to himself as he sipped the cold liquid, *a gilded cage indeed and probably bugged up to the eyeballs!*

Stoneham slept well and woke, feeling refreshed, a few minutes after nine. After a quick shower and shave, he went into the kitchen and made a large plate of scrambled eggs and a pot of fresh coffee. Taking the breakfast tray into the lounge he switched on the TV and was surprised to see it had access to several Western channels. He finished his food then watched the news on CNN. At precisely ten o'clock there was a knock at the door. Not bothering to rise, he shouted, 'Come in.'

The door opened and Hana Chang entered, but not dressed as the day before in a designer business suit. Today she wore the full blown uniform of a colonel in the North Korean military.

'You off to a fancy dress party?'

She ignored the sarcasm. 'Good morning, Greg. How did you sleep?'

He stood up. 'Yeah fine. Okay, when do I get t'find out what this is all about?'

'Very soon, and if you are ready, we can go now'

'Sounds good, let's do it.'

She opened the door and said, 'After you.'

In the corridor two heavily armed soldiers, snapped smartly to attention as Colonel Chang appeared.

Outside, the morning was bright with a cool breeze coming in from the Taedong River. Two Russian made 4x4's, with blacked out windows, and engines running, waited for the colonel and her Western guest to arrive. The waiting soldiers came to attention as the colonel left the building. The rear door of the second vehicle was held open by a young sergeant, who saluted smartly as Stoneham and Chang climbed in.

'All this security really necessary?' said Stoneham.

'Not really,' said Hana quietly. 'We could have travelled into the city quite easily in a cab. But that would never be allowed I'm afraid.'

He grinned at the thought and then turned his attention to the view through the window, as the tiny convoy pulled out of the base.

Chapter Four
'The General'

Kim Il-Sung Square is a massive area in the centre of the city, probably most likened to Red Square but decidedly bigger. Many imposing government buildings surround the square, each more impressive than the one before, with huge columns and magnificent porticos that contradict the ideal of a nation for the people. There is opulence here, but not for the proletariat.

Stoneham smiled at the size of the massive national flags blowing steadily in the late morning breeze, and said, 'You guys got a bit of an identity crisis, Hana?'

She turned to him and then looked up to the huge flags waving above the government buildings. His attempt at humour was not lost on her. 'In America you do not fly your flag on all buildings?'

'I guess so, but ours aren't usually as big as a tennis court.'

As the small convoy pulled up to the rear parking area of one of the buildings. Chang said, 'Okay, we're here.'

The attendant soldiers all dismounted the vehicles and stood to attention as Colonel Chang and the foreigner went into the building. There was no security scanner or staff at the entrance other than a small reception desk, from which a burly uniformed sergeant nodded to Chang as she passed. A large elevator took them to the tenth floor at the top of the building and, on exiting, they were met by a young woman, again in military uniform. After saluting she said, 'Good morning, Colonel, he's waiting for you now.'

The office was huge with a large modern desk in the corner. On the far wall was an oversized portrait of the Supreme Leader and the big windows looked out onto Kim Il-Sung Square. There was a smell of air freshener and cigarette smoke.

The old man behind the desk stood as Chang and Stoneham entered. He wore the uniform of a general and on his chest were at least two dozen medals and insignia. Hana came to attention and snapped a smart salute, which was returned in a very casual manner by the senior officer. The general smiled and walked to the centre of the room. Hana, still at attention said, 'Good morning, General.'

'Good morning, Colonel Chang. Stand at ease.'

Hana turned to the American. 'This is Mr Gregory Stoneham, sir.'

The General held out his hand. 'A pleasure to meet you, Mr Stoneham.'

Stoneham shook hands and smiled slightly, 'You too, General. Please call me Greg, sir.'

The old man turned to Hana, leaned in close and hugged her, then kissed her check. 'It's good to have you back.' The look of surprise on the American's face amused the old man. 'Your military is not as informal as this, Greg?'

'Definitely not, sir.'

General Chang grinned. 'No, nor are we,' then he turned to Hana and touched her arm lightly. 'You see, Greg, Colonel Chang here, is my daughter.'

Stoneham got the joke and smiled. 'Very good, sir. Very good.'

The old man looked at the cane. 'Please forgive my indelicacy, but I see you have a slight limp. Before we continue, are you sure you are up to the challenge we have for you?'

Stoneham looked the general straight in the eyes. My leg does not affect my brain, sir, and that works just fine.'

'Yes of course, excuse me for mentioning it. What happened to your leg? If you don't mind me asking.'

'An accident, the leg was broken and was set rather badly.' Stoneham had a sudden flashback to the girl in the farmhouse, then said, 'The limp is a legacy.'

The general pointed to a pair of couches next to the big windows. 'I see. Well let's take the weight off it and have a seat shall we.'

The old man sat down and took a cigarette from a silver box on the table next to him, picked up a matching silver table lighter and lit the cigarette.

'Now, Greg, cast your mind back to March 2003, the invasion of Iraq. The American coalition forces cross the Kuwaiti border and stream north into Iraq. Saddam's army in the desert is overwhelmed by the tsunami of American tanks and support troops. The Iraqi's are no match for the might of the coalition force and are overrun.'

The old general took another draw on the foul smelling Russian cigarette. 'In Baghdad the battle for air supremacy rages, *Shock and Awe*, as you Americans so colourfully called the bombing of the capital.'

The general coughed, his hand to his mouth, then said, 'British SAS teams throughout the city laser-mark key targets. Military and government buildings, as well as several of Saddam's palaces are all destroyed by the Tomahawk missiles launched from American ships in the Gulf.'

Stoneham was beginning to feel uncomfortable, not knowing where the conversation was going, but sat and listened to the old man.

The general coughed again, took another long draw on the disgusting cigarette and continued his story. 'In his presidential bomb shelter, under the Republican Palace, Saddam Hussain met with his three sons.'

'Scuse me, General, but Saddam only had two sons,' said Stoneham, a puzzled look on his face.

The old man smiled and stubbed out the cigarette. 'Two legitimate sons, yes, but several illegitimate as well.'

Stoneham nodded.

The general coughed again. 'Saddam, his eldest son Uday and his brother Kusay were meeting with Abdullah Hamoud, the illegitimate son by his favourite mistress, Mariana Hamoud. A rare beauty I'm led to believe.' The old man smiled wistfully.

Colonel Chang moved disapprovingly in her seat, and the general returned to his story. 'The reason behind the invasion was of course to secure Iraq's weapons of mass destruction.'

'Scuse me again, sir,' said Stoneham, 'which of course we all know never existed.'

The general smiled again. 'That's not strictly true, Greg. You see Saddam's scientists, his biochemical experts to be precise, were working on a virus. Saddam knew he was years away from a nuclear capability, but a chemical WMD was within reach. Unfortunately for him the invasion came and he was out of time. The pathogen still needed refining, so Saddam planned to get the virus out of Iraq and use it if the war was lost. He would develop the bacteria and use it to take back his country at a later date.'

Stoneham leaned forward, fascinated with the general's story. 'And did he get the pathogen out?'

The old man smiled. 'That was the purpose of the meeting in the bunker. Abdullah Hamoud was tasked with getting the virus, along with all the data, out of the country. He left that very night. There were tunnels out of the palace, to the edge of the Tigris River; Hamoud and two trusted Republican Guard officers took a fast boat out of the city, as the bombs were falling all around them. They made their escape and sailed north to Syria, where they went into hiding.'

Stoneham was fascinated and said, 'So what happened to them and the pathogen?'

The old man stood up, went to the window and looked out into the square. 'Our agents in Syria eventually managed to contact them, and brought them to North Korea.'

'And the virus?' said Stoneham.

'We of course now have the virus and all the data. Well . . ., we had the original virus, but over the years we have refined it and manufactured an antidote.' He turned back and looked at the American. 'We now feel it is time to use it. And that's where you come in, Greg.'

Chapter Five
'Doctor Moon'

The Peoples National Research Centre is located in the outskirts of Pyongyang and sits in a picturesque site on the west bank of the Taedong River. The complex of modern buildings, surrounded by lush parkland, looks like the headquarters of any multinational corporation, but the outward appearance certainly belies the sinister nature of what goes on inside. Heavily armed dog patrols monitor the perimeter and the entrance is manned by several security personnel. CCTV cameras are everywhere.

Stoneham and Chang's small convoy slowly drove up to the main gatehouse. After dismounting the vehicles everyone was subject to the stringent security procedure and even Colonel Hana Chang was thoroughly searched by a female officer. The attendant soldiers in Hana's escort were taken to a small anteroom to wait, while their colonel and the westerner were given visitor badges and then driven off in a small golf buggy by two of the gate security staff.

On entering the building the colonel and Stoneham were again subject to a security screening, albeit not as rigorous as the previous one. A smart young man in a crisp white laboratory coat met them at the security desk.

'Good afternoon, Colonel Chang. My name is Kim Sung. I am a senior research assistant at the facility and will be your escort while you are with us today.'

Hana Chang nodded and said, 'Thank you.' She did not introduce Stoneham.

'If you will follow me please, I'll take you to Doctor Moon.'

There was no sound in the corridors except for the faint noise of the air-conditioning and the tap, tap, tap, of Stoneham's cane on the tiled floor. After passing through several security doors they entered a brightly lit hallway. A young female in civilian clothes stood up from a small desk. She smiled and said, 'Good afternoon,' then opened the door next to her. 'Your guests have arrived, Doctor.'

Kim Sung stood to one side as the secretary showed the visitors into Moon's office.

After the secretary left and closed the door, Hana Chang said, 'Good afternoon, Doctor. Thank you for seeing us.' She did not introduce Stoneham.

'Please have a seat,' said the bespectacled Moon, pointing to a large circular table in the corner of the office.

Hana smiled slightly. 'You have been fully advised of what we require today, Doctor Moon?'

The doctor nodded and returned a nervous smile. 'Yes, Colonel.'

Stoneham was surprised to see the items arrayed on the table and looked enquiringly at Chang. Her expression gave nothing away and she leaned back in her chair. 'Please proceed, Doctor.'

Moon cleared his throat and said, 'The pathogen we received from the Iraqis was a particularly deadly bacterium they had managed to develop. Unfortunately the problem they had was the basic chemistry was extremely unstable and therefore they were unable to produce an effective antidote.' The doctor removed his spectacles and continued. 'We, on the other hand have spent the last few years modifying the virus and manufacturing a suitable antidote.'

Stoneham leaned forward and rested his elbows on the table. 'What does it do, Doctor?'

'Yes, yes, good question. You are familiar with the Ebola and Lassa viruses?'

Stoneham nodded sagely. 'Yes of course.'

'Well, unlike these two haemorrhagic pathogens which as I'm sure you know cause severe bleeding, as well as many other dreadful side effects, our virus is somewhat more sophisticated.' Moon returned his spectacles to the end of his stubby nose and continued. 'Our virus, which we have called the Baghdad bacterium, initially presents the effects of mild asthma. The victim's condition will then deteriorate over a period of seven to ten days into a full blown pneumonic condition which, of course, is one hundred percent fatal, unless the antidote is administered.'

'Jesus,' said Stoneham.

'Jesus himself would not be able to help without the antidote,' said Moon, irreverently.

'How is it spread?'

'Another good question,' said the doctor, as if talking to a student. 'Initially in the water system and then, as each subject is infected, they themselves carry the virus and spread it through any form of physical contact.'

'So it's not an airborne bacterium?' said Stoneham.

'No. We purposefully countered this, as we did not want it to get into the atmosphere.'

The American nodded. 'And how is it transported and introduced into target water supplies?'

The doctor pushed his spectacles back into place and smiled broadly. 'Ah, now that is where we have been very clever, if I may say so.' He pulled a small chrome tray towards him, on which were several white lozenges; not unlike soluble antacid tablets, each wrapped in a cellophane packet. He picked up one and handed it to Stoneham. 'That is the Baghdad bacterium.'

The startled American immediately dropped it back on the tray. 'Jesus Christ!'

Moon almost laughed at the reaction from his visitor. 'There is nothing to worry about when the virus is in this state, although it would be unwise to unwrap it and then lick your fingers.'

Stoneham shook his head slightly and looked at Colonel Chang, who'd been sitting back from the table the whole time. 'Have you seen this before?'

'Yes,' she said, 'well, actually I haven't seen the end product, but I've been fully briefed on the production and how the virus is distributed. It is quite safe in this form.'

'Let's hope so,' said the American. 'And the antidote?'

Moon pulled another chrome tray towards him and picked up a Ziploc bag containing what looked like small barley sugar sweets. 'This is the antidote.'

'Sugar candy?' said Stoneham.

'Quite so,' said Moon. 'To all intents and purposes it does indeed look like sugar candy and actually does taste similar, although with a slightly bitter aftertaste.'

For the first time since entering Moon's office Stoneham smiled. 'So you have a deadly virus that looks like an antacid tablet and an antidote that looks like sweets from a candy store?'

'Precisely,' said the doctor. 'Safe and easy to transport and with the appearance of a couple of innocent everyday items.'

'What about initial dosage, into say, a city reservoir?'

'Yet another very good question,' said Moon, then pointing to the small tray, said in a matter-of-fact way. 'These few tablets would be enough to infect a reservoir servicing a hundred thousand people.'

Chapter Six
'Mercenaries Don't Come Cheap'

Stoneham did not speak until he and Chang were back in the vehicle. 'That is one sick fuck,' he said quietly.

Hana Chang turned to him, a surprised look on her beautiful face. 'I beg your pardon?'

'Moon,' said Stoneham. 'Doctor fucking Moon,' the name was spat out with obvious distaste. 'Smiling away at his handiwork. Talking about how he's made a tablet that could kill thousands of people.'

Colonel Chang continued to look him in the eyes. 'I did not expect you to be so squeamish, Greg. I was led to believe you were a very ruthless man?'

'That's as maybe, but I don't grin like an idiot when talking about mass murder.'

She frowned. 'I hope we have picked the right man for this job, Greg?

He returned her stare. 'You picked the right man. Don't worry. For twenty million dollars, you picked the right man.'

Her smartphone beeped, ending the somewhat tense moment. She looked at the display and then swiped the screen. 'Yes, General . . . That's correct, sir . . . Of course, sir. . .
Goodbye, General.'

Stoneham grinned slightly. 'Daddy?'

'General Chang. Yes,' she said respectfully.

'Okay, where're we off to now?'

'Now, Mr Stoneham we need to discuss what we are going to do with the Baghdad virus. And we need to hear your plan.'

He looked at her for a few seconds and said. 'I need a day or two to think about it. I also need to think about the assets I'm gonna need.'

'We have excellent people you can use, Greg.'

'No thanks, Colonel. I'll set up my own team.'

'Very well, I will discuss that with the general.'

'I use my own people or it's a deal breaker.'

Her dark eyes narrowed. 'Have you forgotten what I told you in Istanbul? This is an all or nothing deal, Greg. You are in now, or . . . '

'Yeah, yeah, I get it,' he interrupted. 'Just make sure you convince General Daddy the job works better if I use my own assets.'

She smiled. 'I will do my best.'

'Oh, and by the way. Anyone else I use will be paid for by you. Not from my fee.'

Her smile faded. 'Of course, Greg, of course.' he heard her sigh as she turned to watch the boats on the Taedong River. Then quietly she said, 'Mercenaries don't come cheap.'

Three days later the diplomatic jet, carrying Colonel Chang and Greg Stoneham touched down at Vladivostok. This old Russian city is a little over eighty miles from the North East border of North Korea and although most of the western world imposes stringent punitive sanctions on the rogue nation, the relationship with neighbouring Russia is amicable, and with their VIP diplomatic papers, entry into Russia was relatively simple for them.

The last few days however had been anything but simple, especially for Stoneham. He'd formulated an initial plan within twenty four hours of the meeting with Doctor Moon and, with Colonel Chang in attendance; he'd outlined the scheme to her father, General Chang, and two other high ranking state security officers. A further twenty four hours had passed while heated discussions were made over the use of Stoneham's own people for the missions.

The protracted deliberations eventually ended positively, thanks to Hana convincing her father to agree. The agreement though had one non-negotiable caveat, which pissed Stoneham off no end. Colonel Hana Chang was to be totally involved with each element of the mission and was to accompany the American every step of the way.

Before they left Pyongyang, several things happened. Firstly, they'd both been given fake identities. Passports and credit cards had been provided in the names of Samuel Healy, a Canadian business man, and his Thai wife, Lilly. Second, and more important as far as Stoneham was concerned, was the first tranche of his fee, being two million dollars, had been transferred to his Montenegro bank account. Next, an operational account to fund the mission had been set up for Stoneham with a private Moscow bank and an initial sum of three million dollars deposited. Lastly he was provided with, and impressed by, a highly encrypted satellite phone that would enable him to make and receive calls without the CIA, MI6, or anyone else for that matter, being able to listen in.

On arrival into Vladivostok they were met by the North Korean Vice Consul and, after a swift transition through the diplomatic channel, were driven to the Consulate.

Situated almost on the beach, the Consulate overlooks the aptly named, Golden Horn Bay. The main building is actually no more than a large villa and although comfortable, does not have the imposing stature of many of the other diplomatic establishments in the neighbourhood.

From the moment she stepped out of the limousine, Colonel Hana Chang was fawned over by the resident Consul, who of course was well aware of her father's position in the NK government. He was however slightly put-out when Chang failed to introduce the limping man with her. That said, he was more than delighted to provide the best hospitality possible to the couple while in his charge, but would be only too happy to see the back of them the following day, when they took the Aeroflot flight to Moscow.

Chapter Seven
'No One Pays Any Attention To Junkies'

The flight time from Vladivostok to Moscow is almost eight and a half hours. With a time difference of seven hours, Aeroflot flight A781 would leave Vladivostok at eight-thirty and would land at Domodedovo, Moscow's second major airport, a little before ten o'clock the same morning.

Stoneham was disappointed to find there was no First Class facility on the plane but thankfully, the Business Class cabin, unlike Economy, was relatively quiet with only a few wealthier Muscovites returning to the capitol.

It had become clear Hana Chang did not like him and the time with her was going to be less pleasant than he originally hoped. That said, he was being paid twenty million dollars, so having to put up with the woman was not an issue and, being a looker, she was no strain on the eye.

The first hour or so of the flight was taken up with the breakfast service, which Stoneham found to be enjoyable and, with a few glasses of Champagne, the journey had started well. After they'd eaten however, the colonel had reclined her seat, slipped on her headphones and became enthralled with one of the inflight movies.

Stoneham read a couple of the English written magazines and then he too reclined his seat and covered himself with the thin blanket provided. He closed his eyes, but sleep never came. Instead his mind went back over the last three years since his fortuitous escape in Panama and how he'd hit back at the Americans and the Brits. His simultaneous attacks on their two security centres in Washington and London had been a monumental embarrassment for the respective services, never mind the personnel they'd lost. The body count was impressive, but their credibility had been brought into question, if only for a few weeks, as they were pilloried in the media. Stoneham smiled to himself, but was drawn from his thoughts by the pretty stewardess asking if he wanted more Champagne.

'Sure, honey and bring me some peanuts, pretzels, or something would you?'

A few minutes later the girl returned with his drink and snack. She smiled at the bald passenger with the crooked nose and said. 'Anything else, sir?'

'I'm good for now,' he looked at her name tag. 'Thank you, Katarina.'

He finished his wine and slipped back into the recline position. Chang was still deep in concentration watching her movie. He closed his eyes again and tried to sleep but his mind, as before, went back to events over the three years since gaining his freedom.

The devastating attacks on the headquarters of the CIA and MI6 had been sponsored by a couple of his clients in the wider terrorist fraternity and he personally had been paid almost three million dollars for planning and executing those attacks. But he'd used almost half of that to fund his own campaign against the Brits and Americans. It cost money to move around the world, especially covertly, but it had been worth it in his eyes. His campaign had been relentless and, with a little help from a couple of other equally anti-American contacts, they'd shot, stabbed, strangled, or blown up, almost three dozen agents and assets across the globe.

This would be his last job and, with twenty million dollars going into the bank, he could now disappear for good. Facial surgery and a totally new identity could be had in South America, and then he was gone. Greg Stoneham would be history.

When Stoneham and Chang had boarded the plane in Vladivostok they used diplomatic papers, but on arrival in Moscow they presented their fake passports to the Border Control and entered the country as Mr and Mrs Healy. The American had arranged for one of his low level Moscow contacts to provide transport. As they came out of the Arrivals Hall, Greg saw the man waiting next to the main exit.

'There's my guy,' he said.

The appearance of the weedy little man waiting for them surprised Hana Chang. In his early thirties, with bloodshot eyes and greasy, unkempt hair, he looked as if he was homeless. Dressed in ripped jeans and a leather jacket, with dirty trainers, she wondered why the very slick Stoneham would use such a person.

Frowning she said, 'He's your contact? He looks like a drug addict.'

Stoneham smiled slightly, leaned close to her ear, and said quietly, 'Don't let his appearance fool you. That's the point. In Moscow no one pays any attention to junkies.'

Chapter Eight
'The Safe House'

It took almost three hours to get from Domodedovo, across the city and north out of Moscow, to the tiny village of Iksha. Situated on the western shore of Lake Pestovski, the old dacha was not large, but certainly impressive, with large double gates and a high wall surrounding it. The once well-kept gardens had now become overgrown and the place looked as if no one had been there for quite some time.

As they climbed out of the car, Hana said, 'What is this place?'

Stoneham didn't answer her, but turned to the junkie-looking driver. 'Is everything okay inside?'

The driver nodded, 'Sure, boss. All ready for you. Here's the keys.'

Stoneham took the small bundle of keys and said, 'Okay see you tomorrow.'

The driver grinned. 'Sure, boss.' He looked at the woman, then to Stoneham, gave a salacious wink and said, 'See you tomorrow.'

Chang and Stoneham watched as the car drove away, then she said. 'I asked you, what is this place?'

'It's a safe house,' he said. 'Come on.'

As they climbed the short flight of wooden steps, the tap, tap, tap, of the wolf's head cane was the only sound to be heard. No wind, no birds, not even the creak of floor boards as they walked to the large double doors. He fiddled with the bundle of keys as she looked at the overgrown gardens. After a few seconds, the door hinges creaked behind her and she turned and followed him into a large entrance hall.

'Oh . . .,' she said.

'Yeah, not bad eh?'

The place was spotlessly clean with a faint smell of furniture polish. It was obvious someone had spent time getting the old house ready for them. The furniture was old but very stylish and the polished wooden floors reflected the sunlight coming in through the open front door.

'You want some coffee or something stronger?' said Stoneham.

She walked into the large drawing room. 'I'd like some tea, please.'

They went into the kitchen and found the cupboards and refrigerator well stocked. He took a beer from the fridge, as she filled a kettle and placed it on the stove.

'You still haven't said what this place is, Greg?'

'I told you. It's a safe house.'

'Whose safe house?'

He drank from the bottle and then said, 'It belongs . . . belonged, to a contact of mine. A guy I used to do business with.'

'Belonged?'

'Yeah. He's dead now.'

As the water boiled the kettle began to whistle. Chang stood up, took it from the flame and continued. 'Was he a close friend?'

'Not really. He was an arms dealer. A pretty big one actually, worked with a lot of the radical organisations around the world. He was assassinated on the steps of Vauxhall Cross in 2009.'

She turned from the stove. 'Vauxhall Cross, the headquarters of the British Security Service?'

'Yeah. Shot right in front of the CIA team who'd just collected him from the Brits. They'd just picked him up and were walking him to the cars when a sniper killed him right in front of them.'

'I heard about this,' she said. 'The reports we got were that he'd managed to get hold of an agent's weapon and killed himself.'

Stoneham shook his head and grinned. 'That was the story they put out to the media, but he was shot by an Israeli agent.'

'Mossad killed him?'

Stoneham finished his beer and said, 'They sure did.'

'What was the arms dealer's name again?'

'Shahadi. Vini Shahadi.'

Chapter Nine
'Hello Lilly'

The previous day had past slowly, with nothing to do other than wait until Stoneham's assets showed up.

Soon after arriving, Hana Chang had made a sat-phone call to the general, her father. The conversation had been entirely in Korean, much to the annoyance of Stoneham, as he'd no idea of what was said. She'd then settled in to one of the five bedrooms and, after finding several books in the drawing room, past the rest of the day reading an English version of Anna Karenina.

Stoneham had made a very nice lunch for them both, after which, as there seemed little chance of any small talk, had walked down to the lake edge where he found an old rowing boat. Although it looked like it was ready to sink, it was actually seaworthy and once he found the oars, he'd spent the rest of the afternoon out on the water.

Today though, was not going to be as restful. The junkie-looking driver was due back around midday with the rest of Stoneham's team and the American was now itching to get the missions underway.

It was almost one o'clock when the car drove through the gates of the dacha. On the steps of the old house

Stoneham and Chang watched as the three men climbed out of the vehicle. The junkie-looking driver scurried to the boot and took out a couple of pieces of luggage.

The appearance of the two new arrivals surprised Chang. Both in their early fifties, one dressed in what looked like an expensive three piece suit, the other wore designer jeans and a blazer. *They look more like business men than mercenaries*, she thought.

The suited man carried a smart briefcase and the other, what looked like a laptop bag.

Stoneham limped down the steps to greet his team, the cane tap, tap, taping, on the wooden steps. Hana Chang watched as hands were shaken and embraces given. The driver scuttled up the steps with the luggage and dropped the bags at the front door. He grinned and winked at her before returning to the three men next to the car.

'Okay, boss.' He said. 'I'll be back same time tomorrow to pick you guys up.'

She watched as Stoneham leaned close to the grinning driver, but she couldn't hear what was said. The look on the driver's face changed and he nodded respectfully to the American, then quickly climbed into the vehicle and drove away.

The three men joined her on the porch and Stoneham made brief introductions. Turning to the man in the blazer he said, 'This is Shaun. Shaun this is Lilly.'

She smiled and said, 'Hello.'

'Hello, Lilly.' The lilting accent was clearly Irish.

Stoneham put his hand on the suited man's shoulder. 'And this is an old colleague of mine, Dushan. Dushan, meet Lilly.'

Again she smiled and shook hands.

'Nice to meet you, Lilly.'

She couldn't place the accent exactly, but knew it was East European.

'Let's get a drink,' said Stoneham, as he pushed the door open with his cane. 'Then we have a lot to go over before we leave tomorrow.'

Chapter Ten
'Who's Dushan Grasic?'

The Massachusetts Institute of Technology is probably the world's most prestigious university for research and education in physical sciences and engineering.

Robert Anderson had taken a double first in computer science and technology at this most august of colleges. The day after his graduation he was approached by, and offered a position with, America's National Security Agency. That had been two years ago.

Robbie wasn't an athlete, nor was he particularly gifted at social interaction. He was somewhat of a loner with little outside interests. His work with the NSA was all consuming and meant everything to him. He was a pleasant enough young man and although not one for associating with his fellow work colleagues, he was indeed highly respected by them. Anderson had been recruited by the NSA not just for his academic achievements, but for his exceptionally analytical brain and more importantly, his photographic memory.

Although not that interesting to most people, Robbie's work was the most important thing in his life. His role was to monitor the down-feeds from three of the many spy satellites the United States had spinning around the globe.

Twenty five miles above the earth's surface, S-Nine-Alpha was in its orbit over North-West Russia. Robbie had been working for almost six hours and was rapidly typing up his end of shift report, while he continued to watch the monitor.

'Supervisor!' he called.

His line boss came over and stood behind the eager young man. 'What you got, Anderson?' he said.

Pointing to the screen, Robbie said, 'Look.'

'What am I looking at?'

'This is a location of interest we monitor north of Moscow. It used to be a safe house for a major Mid-Eastern arms dealer.'

The supervisor nodded. 'Like I said. What am I looking at?'

'There's been no movement at this location for almost two years. The place has been deserted according to our intel. But in the last couple of days there have been vehicles and people arriving.'

'Go on,' said the supervisor.

'Just a second, I'll play back the feed . . .' Anderson tapped the screen with his pen. 'Look at these three guys standing next to the property, this guy in the middle.'

His supervisor leaned in closer. 'Okay, I see him. Do we know him?'

Robbie turned to face his boss. 'That's Dushan Grasic.'

'Who's Dushan Grasic?'

'Really? You don't know?' said Anderson. 'Seventeen years ago, during the Bosnian War, Dushan Grasic led a brutal attack on a small village west of Srebrenica. Grasic ordered no-prisoners, and over sixty unarmed men women and children were massacred.'

'Ah, yes of course,' said the supervisor. 'I remember. The UN War Crimes Commission have been looking for this bastard ever since.'

Chapter Eleven
'Level 5 Eyes Only'

In Buckinghamshire, the little station at East Monkton was busy with commuters waiting for the seven o'clock train to London. Jack Castle had only arrived back from Dubai the previous day and he was not too happy about having to go into the city this morning, even to meet his brother Mathew.

In his mid-fifties, Castle was tall, reasonably fit and healthy, although, and according to his wife Nicole, losing a few pounds would not go amiss. He had a wicked sense of humour and an infectious personality which appealed to most people, although recently he was becoming less tolerant and somewhat short tempered.

After fifteen years in the British Army and rising to the rank of captain in the Special Air Service, he'd moved into the world of private security. The company he'd joined all those years ago now belonged to him and with the help of his partner and friend, Tom Hillman; they'd grown the business into a respected international entity.

The last two years however had been interspersed with a couple of covert missions for MI6.

The train pulled into the station and the commuters piled on, scrambling for seats. Jack waited until the small crowd had cleared, then stepped into the carriage and moved quickly forward to his reserved seat in First Class. The journey into the city was delayed by an issue with striking rail workers, so Jack spent the time catching up on emails and messages. By the time he arrived at Mathew's office he was over an hour late.

Mathew Sterling was Jack's younger brother. They'd grown up in the north of England, in a beautiful home on the edge of Lake Windermere. Like Jack, Mathew also joined the army but had trod a different path. He'd initially worked in Military Intelligence and then spent many years as a field operative for MI6. He too rose quickly through the security service and now, based in London's Vauxhall Cross building, he was section chief of the Asia and Middle East desk. For security reasons he'd chosen to use his mother's maiden name and for the last twenty years or so, had been known as Mr. Mathew Sterling.

'Good morning, sir,' said Mathew's secretary, 'nice to see you again.'

'Morning, Victoria. How are you?'

'I'm well, thank you, sir. When you called and said you were going to be late he took another meeting. But he shouldn't be long now.'

Jack smiled. 'Not a problem.'

'Can I get you anything, sir?'

'No thanks, I'm fine.'

Fifteen minutes later, two grim faced young men in smart three piece suits came out of Mathew's office. They failed to acknowledge the secretary's 'goodbye' in their haste to get out. Victoria raised her eyebrows as the two men scurried away, then said to Jack, 'Okay, sir. Please go in.'

Castle knocked on the door and walked straight in. Mathew stood in the centre of his office. The stern look on his face, changed to a broad smile as his brother entered.

'Looks like you upset those two,' said Jack, nodding towards the door.

'Bloody idiots,' said Mathew, 'supposed to be the new breed of agents for god's sake. More like estate agents.'

Jack laughed. 'Sorry I'm late, bro.'

They hugged, then Mathew said, 'Not to worry. Bloody rail strikes are getting to be expected these days. How's the family?'

'Wonderful, thanks. Nicole sends her regards and your god-daughters are getting to be a right couple of little ladies.'

'It's their birthday soon,' said Mathew, 'I can't believe they're two years old already.'

Jack sat down on the big couch by the window. 'Yes, time just flies by. Speaking of time, what's the rush to see me today? I only got back last night and wanted to spend the day with the family.'

'Yes,' said Mathew, 'I'm sorry about that, but I have a meeting later and I'd like you to come with me.'

Jack looked puzzled, 'A meeting with whom?'

Mathew didn't answer, but turned and went to his desk, picked up a leather folder, then joined his brother on the couch. The cover of the file read, LEVEL 5 EYES ONLY.

Jack smiled, rubbed his hands together and said, 'Oooh. Top secret stuff eh?'

Mathew frowned and opened the file. 'Sorry, I didn't ask. Do you want anything before we begin?'

'No, I'm fine thanks,' said Jack, 'what's the problem?'

'Three years ago, May 2009. We were hit with a drone attack that killed and injured a lot of our people in the Terrace Restaurant.'

Jack's look was serious. 'Yes, of course I remember it. A sad day for you guys. Bad enough losing your people, but you were crucified in the media as well.'

Mathew nodded. 'Bloody awful day. Not our finest hour to let that happen. Our cousins in Langley had a bigger body-count than we did. And the stick the American media gave the CIA was relentless. Their director had to resign. He was a good guy and didn't deserve to go.'

'The media loves a scapegoat,' said Jack, sombrely.

Mathew nodded and flicked through the papers in the folder. 'That was three years ago. Since then, MI6 has lost several agents and assets on a regular basis. Not since the Cold War has there been such attrition.'

Jack leaned forward. 'How many is, several?'

Mathew turned over a couple more pages and read. 'Far East, three. Central Asia, two. Middle East, three. Russia, four. America, two.'

'Jesus, Matt. That's one every couple o' months.'

'Yes, and I'm told the Americans have lost even more. It's not unheard of to lose an agent or asset, but not at this rate.'

'So what the hell is going on?'

Mathew closed the file and placed it on the table. 'MI6 and the CIA are being targeted.'

Chapter Twelve
'Reciprocity'

Mathew and Jack left the underground parking area of Vauxhall Cross a couple of minutes before midday. The traffic as usual was horrendous, and in any other vehicle it would have taken at least thirty minutes to get from the Embankment to Grosvenor Square. This morning however, thanks to their police motorcycle outrider and their very accomplished driver, the big Jaguar pulled up to the rear entrance of the American Embassy as Big Ben chimed the quarter hour.

A burly security officer came out of the small gate house and even though he recognised the car, and Mathew, he still asked for ID's.

A second guard walked around the vehicle pushing a large mirror on wheels and checked the underside of the Jaguar.

Documents returned, the burly guard said, 'Thank you, sir. One moment please.'

In front of the vehicle three large steel bollards sank quickly into the road and the heavily fortified gate silently swung open.

'Okay, sir. Go ahead. Usual visitors zone, please'

A golf buggy with two security escorts preceded them to the parking area. The driver and police escort remained with their vehicles as Jack and Mathew were taken into the rear of the Embassy. As they were undergoing the security screening a tall American in a dark pinstripe suit approached. 'Mathew, great to see you.'

The pair shook hands, then the American turned to Jack. 'Mr Castle, sir. Good to see you again.'

Jack nodded. 'Yes, hello again.' Jack couldn't remember the man's name, but Mathew came to the rescue. 'How are you, Stephen?'

The tall American smiled. 'I'm good. Was hoping to get home to the States for a vacation, but this latest issue has put a stop to that.'

'Yes, indeed,' said Mathew, sympathetically.

'Okay,' said the American, 'the chief's waiting for you, gentlemen. This way please.'

The office was not big, but did look out over the small park in the centre of Grosvenor Square. Stella Grayson stood as the three men entered. She looked younger than her forty five years, with short blonde hair that framed a pleasant friendly face, and in her dark grey skirt and pale grey silk blouse looked more like a secretary than the Head of Station for the CIA in London.

She came from behind the desk and said, 'Mathew, good to see you again.'

'Good afternoon, ma'am,' said Sterling, as they shook hands.

'And, Jack, always nice to see you too. How is that lovely family of yours?'

'Thank you, ma'am, they are all very well.'

She nodded towards a group of chairs around a small coffee table. 'Please have a seat, gentlemen,' then turned to the tall American. 'Thank you, Stephen, that'll be all for now.'

As the door closed, Grayson said, 'Thanks for coming over, Mathew. I hope the traffic wasn't too tiresome.'

He smiled. 'Not a problem, ma'am. Not with one of London's finest out in front.'

She smiled. 'Ah, yes, of course. Okay, let's begin. As you know, both our organisations have had a serious problem with asset loss over the last few years and, although we have all taken steps to protect our people, we still continue to loose valuable agents.'

Jack thought to himself. *She talks about them as if they were staff in a bloody insurance company, not real people who've been slaughtered.*

Mathew took a bottle of water from the table. 'May I?'

The woman nodded as Sterling cracked the seal and poured half the contents into a glass.

She cleared her throat and continued. 'We have recent intel which may help us with that. Unfortunately it may also indicate we have a bigger issue on the horizon.'

She stood up and went to her desk, picked up a red leather folder, and returned to her seat. Jack and Mathew sat silently for a few seconds while the CIA chief flicked through the documents.

'One of our sharp-eyed NSA guys picked this up a few days ago.' Grayson passed a black and white A4 photograph to Mathew.

As he put on his glasses, he said, 'This is a still from one of your satellite feeds?'

She nodded. 'That's right, from a bird in orbit over North-West Russia. The location is just outside a remote village on the banks of Lake Pestovski, north of Moscow.'

Mathew nodded. 'Okay.'

Grayson looked at the MI6 chief. 'You don't look surprised, Mathew?'

He looked over the rim of his spectacles. 'Sorry, go on, ma'am.'

'You're looking at a terrorist safe house, Mathew. And according to our analyst, the subject in the middle of that little group is definitely Dushan Grasic.'

Sterling turned to the woman. 'The Bosnian war criminal?'

She nodded. 'The very same.' she studied his face. 'Have you seen this snapshot before, Mathew?'

'No, ma'am.'

Sterling squinted slightly and held the photograph closer. 'Have you identified the other two men?'

Grayson didn't take her eyes off him, watching his expression. She sensed he was playing his cards close to his chest. 'One we couldn't identify, but the bald one is of high interest to us. We could only pick up a partial view of his face and he is clearly not as we knew him.' She leaned forward and tapped the picture. 'You see he's using a walking cane now?'

Sterling nodded, and then looked at the woman. 'So you do know him, ma'am?'

'We believe so,' said Grayson. 'And so do you, gentlemen.'

Mathew handed the photo to his brother. After several seconds Jack said, 'Okay?'

'As I said, we only got a partial view of his features, but our facial recognition software suggests a ninety percent possibility that the bald man in the picture is Greg Stoneham.'

Mathew sat back in his seat, silent for several seconds. He looked at the woman across from him and smiled ever so slightly. 'Reciprocity,' he said.

She looked at him, eyes narrowed. 'Mathew?'

He picked up his crocodile skin briefcase and placed it on the table.

'Nice case,' she said, 'Ferragamo?'

Mathew looked a little sheepish. 'A gift from my brother.'

Jack smiled.

Mathew took the EYES ONLY folder from the elegant piece of luggage and said again, 'Reciprocity. Something for something.'

'I'm familiar with the expression, Mathew. What do you have?' said Grayson.

He opened the folder, removed a couple of sheets of paper and handed them to the CIA chief. 'This confirms your intel and identifies the third man in your snapshot, ma'am.'

Grayson speed-read through the documents then looked up. 'Shaun Maguire?'

'Not exactly,' said Sterling.

She shook the papers in her hand and said, 'This says Shaun Maguire, Dushan Grasic and Greg Stoneham met a few days ago in Russia.'

Sterling picked up his glass and finished the water. 'Maguire, as I'm sure you know, was jailed several years ago for his part in the planning of the London bombings.'

Grayson nodded. 'Yes, I wasn't here at the time, but I read a report on the atrocity and who was involved.'

Mathew removed his spectacles and rubbed the bridge of his nose. 'Maguire was sentenced to nineteen years and incarcerated in Belmarsh maximum security prison.'

Grayson raised her eyebrows and said, 'And you guys let him escape a year ago.'

'Not exactly,' said Sterling, 'you see, ma'am, Shaun died of a heart attack just over a year ago. There was no family or friends to notify and he was cremated without ceremony.'

Grayson sat back in her seat and smiled. 'So you guys bring in your own man to play the part of Shaun Maguire. It was your guy who allegedly escaped.'

'Yes, ma'am. And for the last year he's been getting closer and closer to a contract terrorist, who we now know to be Greg Stoneham.'

'Well done, Mathew, well done.'

Jack smiled at the CIA chief's comment. *One up for us*, he thought.

Mathew put his glasses back on and looked at his documents. 'We believed the attacks on MI6 and the CIA could have been personal. And one of the main individuals who had an axe to grind was Greg Stoneham. It was only after he escaped from your people the attacks on our assets began.'

'Touché, Mathew,' she said with a wry smile.

'I didn't mean it that way, ma'am.'

She raised her hand. 'It's fine, Mathew. Please go on.'

'Our man got back into the UK yesterday, came in on a truck from Calais with a bunch of illegals.'

'Very cloak and dagger,' said Grayson.

'Exactly, and just as Stoneham planned.'

'During their meeting in Russia?' asked the CIA chief.

'Yes, ma'am. We have initially de-briefed our man and he reports that Stoneham has planned major attacks on the UK mainland and in America. Shaun Maguire, our guy, was recruited by Stoneham to enter the UK covertly and infect a major water supply with a deadly virus.'

'Jesus Christ,' said Grayson, 'presumably your guy has the virus with him?'

'Yes. It's currently being analysed by our top bio-scientists.

'Does he have the antidote as well?'

'Not as such. But he was inoculated with the antidote before he left Russia.'

'Thank God,' said Grayson, 'so you'll use his blood to identify and hopefully manufacture the antidote?'

'That's correct, ma'am, but all that takes time.'

'Yes, yes, of course,' she said. She stood up, went to the window and looked out over Grosvenor Square Park. 'So the attack on the UK is obviously not going to happen, but what about the States?'

Sterling turned around and looked at the woman. 'Our man reports that Dushan Grasic was tasked with the American attack. But he wasn't privy to the details, as Stoneham briefed each of them separately.'

'Okay, Mathew, this is excellent intelligence, wonderful work by you and your team.'

Jack spoke for the first time since saying hello. 'We feel there's a lot more, ma'am.'

She returned to her seat and looked at Jack. 'Yes?'

Jack looked at Mathew, who said, 'Go ahead, Jack.'

'There was a woman with Stoneham, Asian, maybe Chinese or perhaps Korean. Stoneham introduced her as Lilly'

'Korean?' said Grayson.

Jack nodded. 'Yes, ma'am.'

Mathew handed another sheet of paper to the woman. 'We believe Stoneham has planned three attacks, ma'am.'

She quickly read the document, then looked at Sterling. 'Your guy is sure about this?' she said, as she held up the paper.

'He is. He said he listened to a conversation between Stoneham and this Lilly, and the gist was how they planned to get into Saudi Arabia.'

Chapter Thirteen
'All-American Ronin'

The drive back to Vauxhall Cross was as swift and efficient as the outbound trip. Very little was said between Jack and Mathew while in the car, but once back in Matt's office and with a tray of tea and sandwiches in front of them, the two brothers had plenty to talk about.

Stella Grayson had provided Mathew with a flash-stick loaded with copies of the CIA's files on the rogue agent, Gregory Stoneham.

After the lunch tray was cleared by Victoria, and instructions given to not be disturbed, Mathew took a spare laptop from a drawer and loaded the memory stick.

'Why not use your desk computer?' said Jack.

Mathew smiled wryly. 'Because I don't know what else is on this,' he tapped the piece of plastic sticking in the side of the laptop, 'those sneaky buggers over there could have some Trojan in here, and the last thing I want is for them to have access to my computer. Even if they are our closest allies.'

Jack grinned and nodded, then pulled his chair alongside his brother. As the screen lit up with documents, the two men began to study the career history of the man who had abandoned Jack and his team to die in Syria.

It took the best part of an hour to go through Stoneham's career history, by which time Jack was seriously impressed. It was however unclear why such a staunch and loyal American had gone rogue. It seemed likely it had begun while he was stationed and operating out of Kabul, in Afghanistan, but the reason behind the man's change of allegiance was not evident from the information they had before them.

'Okay,' said Mathew, 'what d'you think?'

Jack returned his chair to the front of his brother's desk, then took a seat on the big couch. The guy is obviously excellent at what he does. Great tactician and planner. Successful covert missions. Black-ops and assassination. He has all the skills to be a world class operative, or a world class terrorist. And now he's the original All-American Ronin.'

Mathew look puzzled. 'What?'

'Ronin,' said Jack, 'a disgraced Samurai, who sells his sword to the highest bidder.'

'Yeah, right,' said Mathew, with a slight smile at his brother's knowledge of all things trivial. 'So we need to think what his next move is gonna be.'

'We?' Jack shook his head slightly and grinned, 'I don't think so bro. There won't be an attack in the UK and the Americans are more than capable of capturing Dushan Grasic. Just pass-on all your intel to the Saudi's, and let them hunt Stoneham in the Kingdom.'

Mathew came from behind his desk and joined his brother on the couch. 'There is no one in the British security services who has more experience, contacts and friends in the Middle East than you, Jack.'

'Oh, you bugger,' said Jack, a wide grin on his face. 'Bloody flattery won't work this time. I am not going to Saudi. My wife would kill me.'

'Nicole knows you as well as I do, Jack. You always want to do the right thing. And to be honest you enjoy it, you always have done, big brother.'

Jack's grin didn't fade. 'Don't, big brother me. I don't really work for you, or MI6.'

'Not officially, no. But you have in the past.'

'I said, no!'

'Well would you at least talk to Shaun Maguire, our guy, I mean? See what you think. Maybe come up with some ideas of what Stoneham's next move is likely to be?'

Jack nodded, 'Yeah, sure. Set up a meet with your fake Shaun and we can have a chat.'

'Thank you, Jack.' Mathew stood and went to his desk, pressed the intercom and said. 'Victoria, please ask him to come in now.'

Jack grinned again, shook his head slightly, and said, 'You bugger.'

'Come in,' said Sterling, in answer to the knock on the door.

His secretary entered and held the door open as the man with her walked in. 'Can I get you anything else, sir?' she said.

'No thanks, Victoria,' said Sterling.

Jack stood as Mathew made the introduction. 'Jack Castle, meet Ryan Lafferty, aka Shaun Maguire.'

'Ryan, this is, Jack.'

'My pleasure, surr.' The lilting accent was definitely Northern Irish.

Jack smiled. 'No need for sir. Call me, Jack.'

'Fair enough . . . Jack.'

Jack studied him for several seconds. Tall, maybe six foot two and built like a man who'd done manual work all his life, but with eyes that showed a deeper intelligence. With his thick head of wavy dark hair and his handsome face, he was every bit the Gaelic charmer.

'Let's have a seat,' said Sterling.

The Irishman sat down on the opposite couch to the two brothers and said, 'Thank you, surr.'

'I know you're still being de-briefed, Ryan, but I wanted us to get together with Jack here, especially as you say Stoneham's third target could be Saudi.'

'Not a problem, surr.'

'You see, Jack is very well experienced in the Middle East.'

Jack cleared his throat. 'Scuse me for interrupting, but enough about me for now. I'm sure Mr Sterling here knows all about your background, but indulge me for a few minutes, Ryan.'

'No problem, surr . . . Jack. What d'you wanna know?'

'Just a potted version will do.'

'Okay . . . I was born in Armagh to a staunch Protestant family. Dad was a builder and my two brothers worked with him. I did too for a couple o' years, and then I joined up.'

'Army?' said Jack.

'Aye. Came over to the mainland and joined the Parachute Regiment. Two years later I'm back in the

Bogside, patrolling the streets with the Para's. Right back where I bloody started.'

Jack grinned. 'So how did you get involved with MI6?'

The Irishman looked at Mathew.

'It's okay, Ryan. You can speak freely in front of Jack.'

'Thank you, surr. When my time was up with the regiment, I was approached by Special Branch. I worked for them for a few years and then moved across to 5.'

'Ah,' said Jack. 'So you worked for MI5 first and then this lot dragged you in.'

'That's right. Apparently I looked as near as damn it to Shaun Maguire as anyone, so I got the job of impersonating him.'

'And you managed to infiltrate Stoneham's circle a year ago?'

'Not quite a year. Took me a coupla month for him to make contact. Well, I say make contact, it was through an intermediary on the Dark-web.'

Jack nodded. 'Hrrrm, the terrorists own messaging system. But you obviously did get a face-to-face with him eventually?'

'Only a few days ago, in Russia. This is the first job he's recruited me for in person, the others were all done via the intermediary.'

'Others?'

Ryan shot another questioning look at Sterling. 'Go on, you can talk,' said Mathew.'

'I did two jobs for him. The first was a hit on a couple of MI6 assets in Asia; the other was an agent in Russia.'

Jack looked shocked for a second, and then saw the Irishman smile . . . 'You stage-managed the hits?'

'Of course. The first was a car bomb. The bomb went off, but the people inside were a couple of bodies from the local morgue, a couple o' poor vagrants. The second was a shooting in St Petersburg. I shot the guy in a packed café, blood everywhere, just like the movies. The ambulance that picked him up was ours. The agent in question is fit and well and now deeper under-cover than he ever was.'

Jack grinned. 'Yeah, just like the movies.'

Lafferty leaned forward in his seat. 'But we still lost plenty of our people and all down to Mr bloody Stoneham.'

'Yes,' said Jack, seriously, 'yes, of course.' Then smiling, he continued. 'You ever come across a guy called Tom Hillman when you were with MI5?'

The Irishman nodded. 'I did indeed. We worked together a coupla times. Then he went into the private sector. Not seen him for years.'

'Tom and I are in business together. He's my partner, and has been a mate for longer than I care to remember.'

'Well, bugger me,' said the Irishman, 'for sure it's a small world.'

'Err, we're getting off-message here, gentlemen,' said Mathew.

'Sorry,' said Jack. 'Okay, back to our friend Stoneham. You believe there is a definite threat to the Kingdom?'

The smile disappeared from the handsome face. 'I do, Jack, and I've a feeling I know what his target could be?'

'Me too.' said Jack. 'The Hajj?'

Lafferty nodded. 'Yeah. In a few days' time there's gonna be over a million people in Mecca. What better place to release the Baghdad virus?'

Chapter Fourteen
'Conversations'

It was after seven when Jack got off the train at East Monkton station. He picked up his car from the small parking area and ten minutes later arrived at the entrance to his drive. He pressed the button on the dashboard and waited a few seconds for the big electric gates to swing open. As he drove slowly up to the house the gates closed behind him. There'd been a light shower earlier and the gardens were still wet from the rain. He got out of the car and stood looking at the beautiful gardens surrounding the house. For several seconds he relished the peace this place always gave him. He sucked in a deep lung-full of fresh clean air, just as his smartphone beeped. He looked at the display and swiped the screen. 'Mathew?'

'Hello, Jack. Are you home yet?'

'Just this minute arrived. What's up, bro?'

'We have the initial analysis of the virus Ryan Lafferty brought us.'

'And?' said Jack

'And there is no virus.'

'Sorry, Matt. What d'you mean?'

'Exactly that. There is no virus, it's fake, a dud, there is no harmful bacteria in the lozenges that Lafferty was given.' The phone was silent for several seconds, and then Mathew said, 'You still there, Jack?'

'Yeah . . . Yes, sorry. What about the antidote? What about the bloodwork you took from Ryan?'

'The same. Nothing in his blood that's out of the ordinary. There's a higher reading for glucose, but nothing unusual. Definitely no antidote.'

'What the hell's going on?' said Jack.

* * *

Two hundred miles away, in the quaint coastal town of Whitby, another conversation was in progress. The bar in the Fisherman's Rest pub was far too noisy to talk, so the two men had gone into the toilets. The older man checked the cubicles, then turned to the other. 'Well? Are you in?'

The young man looked suspicious. 'Fifty quid? Just to smash up an office?'

The other man nodded. 'That's right. You wait until after dark, then give it a good going over.'

The youngster frowned. 'Make it seventy.'

'Okay. Seventy it is. But don't fuck it up. And don't get caught.'

As the cash changed hands, a drunk staggered into the toilet. 'Aye up, lads. Ow's it goin?'

The kid quickly stuffed the money into the pocket of his dirty jeans, winked at his benefactor, then almost knocked the drunk over in his haste to get out.

Chapter Fifteen
'Nicely Done'

Andy Morgan had been a fisherman most of his working life. The last ten years however had seen him in the respected position of Whitby's Harbour Master.

The morning was clear and bright and, through the powerful binoculars, he could see all the way to the horizon. About eight miles out a few local fishing boats nestled on the calm water. As the catch was pulled in, a large flock of seagulls swooped onto the fish laden nets. A container-laden supply boat headed east, on its way to the oil rigs in the North Sea; and a couple of pleasure craft were sailing up the coast, their wakes trailing lazily behind them. Nothing out of the ordinary as far as Andy Morgan was concerned, nothing other than the large sleek motor cruiser being tied up alongside the seawall.

Fifteen minutes later, two men and a very attractive woman walked into Andy's office.

'Good morning,' said Morgan. 'And welcome to Whitby. I'm the Harbour Master.'

The shorter of the two men said, 'Thank you, sir. This is our first point of entry into the UK, so we need to register our arrival, please?'

Morgan nodded to the tall man with the walking cane. Sit down here, sir.'

'I'm fine thank you,' said the tall man. The accent was American,

'Where've you folks come from?' said Morgan.

The man smiled. 'We're out of St Petersburg, on our way to Portugal.'

'Oh, that's a nice voyage,' said Morgan. Then, pointed through the window to the sleek motor vessel moored at the seawall. 'And in that little beauty it should be a very smooth trip.'

'Yes, indeed,' said the man. 'So can we register, please?

Morgan waved his arm, gesturing to the pile of smashed furniture and equipment in the corner. 'Yes of course. But as you can see, we had a spot of trouble last night. Bloody vandals got in and wrecked the place.'

'Oh, that's terrible,' said the man, a look of concern on his face.

'I'm sorry, but the computer was smashed as well, so I won't be able to run your passports. But I can take down your details and, once we're back up and running, I'll input the information in a couple of days.'

'That would be fine,' said the man. 'We've only put into Whitby to stock up on a few supplies and check over the engine.'

'Ah, okay,' said Morgan. 'So how long will you be in port?'

'My engineer says he only needs a few hours on the engine, so we'll probably be leaving this afternoon.'

'Okay, so you're really just in transit?'

'That's correct, sir.'

'Good, that makes things easy. I can take your passport details and stamp you in, and out, of the UK now. Then input in a few days, when the new equipment arrives. But for now, you're entry and exit will be legal, with no immigration problems.'

The man smiled. 'That's very kind. Thank you, sir.'

Morgan returned the smile. 'Your documents, please.'

The man handed over a small stack of passports and the ship's registration logbook. 'That's my passport, three crew members, and these two passengers. And this is the *Kristina's* logbook for you to stamp, please, sir.'

Half an hour later, in the car park of the Fisherman's Rest, Greg Stoneham found the keys behind the front tyre of the car. The lights flashed as he unlocked the vehicle. Colonel Chang opened the boot, dropped in a small holdall, then got in the front passenger seat.

As they drove out of the carpark, Hana Chang turned to her co-conspirator and said, 'Very nicely done, Mr Stoneham. Very nicely done, indeed.'

Stoneham looked at the colonel, gave a slight smirk and switched on the SATNAV. The pre-programmed destination appeared on the screen. The display showed seventy two miles and a travelling time of one hour fifty minutes. As he drove up the steep hill from the harbour, he said, 'If all goes well, we should be back here by eleven o'clock, and underway again before noon.'

Chang nodded, then turned her attention to the big ruined building perched on the clifftop, 'What's that?' she said.

Stoneham took his eyes off the road for a second and glanced at the gothic ruin. 'No idea. Looks like an old ruined castle or something.'

As they approached the top of the hill, the lilting voice from the SATNAV said, *At the end of the road, turn right . . . towards . . . Middlesbrough.*

Chapter Sixteen
'Nothing So Vulgar As A Helipad'

The following morning, the weather in Berkshire was warm, with a few clouds scattered across an otherwise clear blue sky. The breakfast table had been set out on the big patio overlooking the lake. Nicole Orlova-Castle was talking on the phone when Jack came out. He walked up behind her and gently kissed her neck. She turned and smiled, pursed her lips and blew him a kiss, then went on talking. He sat down and picked up the newspaper. A few minutes later she ended the call and said, 'Sorry about that, darling. Just the office.'

'Everything okay, babe?'

'Yes. We have that charity event in Covent Garden in a couple of weeks.'

'Right,' said Jack, 'you mentioned it before. All under control I imagine?'

She poured some coffee and smiled. 'All under control.'

Nicole and Jack had been together for over eighteen years, the last three as husband and wife. Born to a Russian father and English mother, she'd been blessed with the beauty of her late mother and the brains of her oligarch father. Her early career had been as a successful fashion model in Moscow, but now she owned and operated a lucrative chain of high-end spas and beauty salons across the UK. She'd also taken sound advice from her father and diversified into bricks and mortar,

80

resulting in an extensive portfolio of London and European properties.

Jack looked at her over his paper, as she sipped her coffee. *As beautiful now as the day I first met her.* he thought.

'What're you smiling at?' she said.

'You.'

She blew him another kiss, then picked up a glossy magazine.

'It's quiet out here. Where are the girls?' said Jack.

'They'll be down shortly. Svetlana said there's been a bit of an argument over what they want to wear today.'

Jack laughed. 'Jesus, they're only two years old and already fashionistas. I wonder where they get that from?'

As he finished speaking, his twin daughters came running onto the patio.

'No running on the tiles girls,' said the protective nanny.

Jack scooped them up and sat one on each knee. 'Morning, ladies.'

The girls giggled, then reached onto the table to scoop up tiny handfuls of strawberries. He juggled to keep the little ones from escaping. 'Svetlana, could you ask Brian if I can have a word, please?' he said.

'Yes, Mr Jack.'

Brian Walker was ex SAS, and an old employee of Jack's who'd been partially disabled. Since the birth of the twins, Walker, and his wife, Maggie, were now live-in help. Brian served as gardener, handyman, driver and general dogsbody, but most importantly, he was reliable onsite security, for when Jack was away.

A couple of minutes later the gardener arrived. 'Morning, boss, Miss Nicole. Hello girls.'

'Morning, Brian,' said Nicole.

The twins giggled at the big jolly man.

'Mornin, Brian. How're you today, buddy?' said Jack.

'All good. Couple of issues with the lake, but I spoke to Miss Nicole a few days ago about that and we've sorted it out.'

'Okay, well done. Could you get the tennis court ready, please? We have a chopper coming in this morning.'

'Sure, no problem,' said Brian, 'what's the ETA, boss?'

Jack looked at his Rolex. 'Should be here in about an hour. Ten o'clock.'

'Okay, will-do.'

After Brian had gone, Nicole frowned. 'And who might we be expecting this morning, Mr Castle?'

Jack tried to look nonchalant. 'Err . . . Mathew said he needed to meet again. I told him I didn't want to trail all the way into the city and for him to come here.'

'What's he got you involved in now, Jack?'

Jack feigned the nonchalant look again . 'Nothing, babe. Honestly.'

Her beautiful smile reappeared. 'I hope not,' she said. 'Will he be staying for lunch?'

'Don't think so. He's got a lot on his plate these days.'

Nicole got up and took the twin's hands, then leaned down and kissed Jack, causing the girls to giggle. 'I'll tell Maggie anyway, just in case he decides to stay.'

He watched her as she walked back into the house, then wolf-whistled. Nicole looked over her shoulder, winked, and wiggled her backside in response.

It was a few minute before ten when Jack walked down to the tennis court. Brian had dropped the nets and removed the side posts. The Union Flag, which usually flew on the corner flagpole, had been taken down and replaced with a bright orange windsock and the hi-visibility strobe light on top of the pole was flashing. Brian stood at the edge of the tennis court, a short wave radio in hand.

As Jack arrived, Brian said, 'Two minutes, boss.'

Jack nodded and looked towards the sound of the incoming helicopter. A few seconds later it came into view. He smiled to himself at how they had multi-rolled the tennis court, just to accommodate his father-in-law.

Nicole's father, Dimitri Mikhailovich Orlov, the Russian billionaire oligarch, was very close to his only daughter and saw her as much as he could, but since the birth of his two grandchildren the visits had certainly increased. *'You need to put in a helipad, my boy,'* he'd told Jack. Nicole of course had laughed at the idea of something as vulgar as a helipad and it was she who'd come up with the idea of the multifunction tennis court.

The clatter of the Metropolitan Police helicopter coming into land, snapped Jack back to the job in hand.

The engines shut down and the rotors slowly came to a stop. Jack watched as his brother and Ryan Lafferty climbed out of the sleek aircraft and, with heads bowed, the pair jogged to the edge of the court.

'Good morning, Jack,' said Mathew.

'Mornin,' said Lafferty. 'Lovely place you got here, Jack.'

'Coffee?' said Jack, as they set off up to the house.

The three men took seats around the breakfast table. A few minutes later they all stood as Nicole came out. She went straight over to her brother-in-law, kissed his cheek, and said, 'Mathew, lovely to see you again.' Then turning to the Irishman said, 'Hello, I'm Nicole.'

'Ryan Lafferty,' he said offering his hand.

'Nice to meet you, Mr Lafferty.'

Clearly smitten with the beautiful woman in front of him, he said, 'Please call me Ryan.'

Nicole smiled and said, 'Ryan.' She turned back to Mathew. 'Please sit down gentlemen, Fresh coffee and tea will be out in a few minutes and I'll send something down to your pilot. Will you be staying for lunch, Mathew?'

'Unfortunately not. But thanks anyway, Nicole.'

'Okay, I'll leave you boys to your business.'

After Nicole left and Maggie had brought out the tea and coffee, Jack said, 'Okay, Matt, so what's the situation?'

'One of our big-ears people, at GCHQ came up with something yesterday.'

Jack smiled at the nick-name for the operatives at the British Government's monitoring station in Cheltenham. 'Okay?'

'There was a satellite phone call made from the North East of England.'

Jack grinned slightly. 'And what did big-ears hear?'

Mathew caught the grin and frowned. 'That's the problem. Our operative didn't hear anything. The call was encrypted. All we know is there was a sat-phone call made to Pyongyang at twelve-sixteen hours yesterday.'

'North Korea?' said Jack.

'North Korea,' said Mathew.

Jack poured some tea. 'Where in the North East?'

Mathew swallowed a mouthful of coffee. 'Whitby.'

There was silence around the table for several seconds, until Jack said, 'Have you been onto anyone in Whitby? Anything out of the ordinary up there?'

'We have, and there is.'

Jack leaned forward. 'Okay, like what?'

'The Harbour Master's office was vandalised two nights ago and yesterday afternoon a car was set on-fire at the local pub car-park.'

Again there was silence, until Jack said, 'Any strange vessels coming and going?'

'We spoke with the Harbour Master and there was a seagoing cruiser in from St Petersburg, enroute to Portugal.'

'Anything else?' said Jack.

'We got the local police to check the CCTV files from the pub, but apparently the system had been put out of order.'

Jack smiled and looked at Ryan. 'What d'you think, my Irish friend?'

'Someone wanted to get in and out without any immigration checks,' said the Irishman.

Jack nodded, then turned to his brother. 'How d'you fancy a little trip up to the seaside?'

Mathew drained his coffee cup and nodded. 'The flight plan's already been filed.'

'Oh, you, bugger,' said Jack, 'gimme a minute, I'll just let Nikki know I'll be away for the rest of the day. She's gonna give me hell.'

'She'll be fine,' said Mathew.'

Jack frowned. 'You really don't know my wife, do you, Matt?' As he walked back into the house, he said, 'I'll meet you guys down at the chopper.'

Chapter Seventeen
'Dracula Landed Here'

Inspector Bob Waite, watched as the clattering aircraft descended onto the Fisherman's Rest car park. He and his fellow police officers had cleared the cars and were waiting for over an hour for the arrival of the *big-shots* from London.

A small crowd had gathered to see the unprecedented landing. One local wit shouted, 'We nev'r 'ad this much excitement when Dracula landed 'ere.'

Inspector Waite grinned at the reference to Bram Stoker's famous novel, then waved to the three men exiting the aircraft.

'Mr Sterling?' said Waite

Mathew stepped forward and offered his hand, 'I'm Sterling.'

The policeman shook hands. 'Inspector Waite, sir.'

'Thank you for meeting us, Inspector. You're the senior officer here in Whitby?'

'That's right, sir. My boss is based up the road in Middlesbrough, but I'm sure I can help with anything you need.'

'Yes, yes of course. Thank you, Inspector.'

The policeman waited to be introduced to the other two men but, as no introduction was forthcoming, he said, 'The Harbour Master and landlord are in the pub waiting for you, sir.'

Mathew nodded. 'Thank you. I'll talk to them now, please.'

In the corner of the car park, a fire damaged Citroen had been cordoned-off with blue and white police tape. Jack nodded to the vehicle and, as Mathew went off with the inspector, he and Ryan were escorted to the car by a burly police sergeant.

Lafferty looked inside. 'Not too badly damaged at all.'

The sergeant looked at the Irishman, clearly noting the lilting accent. 'No, sir. Thanks to the landlord. He was in the pub's back yard and saw the fire. Got a couple of staff and tackled it with extinguishers. By the time the Fire Brigade arrived it was just a smoking mess.'

'No one's been near it since?' said Jack.

'No, sir. We've had a constable on guard. We didn't want to leave it unattended until the recovery truck came. Bloody kids here would be all over it. Then we got instructions to leave it where it was until you guys arrived.'

Jack smiled and said, 'Right,' then leaned inside and saw the keys in the ignition. He gave them a turn and was pleased to hear the engine kick into life.

Stating the obvious he said, 'We got power.'

'SATNAV?' said Lafferty.

'Checking it now,' said Jack.

The sergeant watched as the two strangers scrolled through the system's information.

'Here it is,' said Jack, 'the last destination.'

'Good,' said the Irishman.

Jack took out his smartphone and photographed the display. 'Okay, that's all we need for now, Sergeant. Thanks a lot.'

'Very good, sir.'

Inside the Fisherman's Rest, the small dining room had been cleared of customers. Mathew was sitting with the inspector and a couple of other men.

The landlord was speaking. 'Aye, we 'ad fire out pretty sharpish. If that bloody thing 'ad blown, we could'a lost pub. We wasn't 'anging aroun' for't bloody Fire Brigade.'

'Okay, thank you, Mr Ross. You've been very helpful, sir,' said Mathew.

'Aye, nae bother. Can'a get you lads owt' t'drink?'

'Maybe later,' smiled Mathew. 'That'll be all for now, Mr Ross.'

'Aye, okay,' said Ross.

After the landlord left, Mathew turned to the Harbour Master. 'Mr Morgan, isn't it?'

'Yes, sir. But please call me, Andy.'

Sterling smiled. 'Okay, Andy. Tell me about the people and the boat that arrived yesterday?'

Chapter Eighteen
'Alpha-One Situation'

The Blackton Reservoir is situated in the foothills of the northern Pennines and supplies water to the main cities in the North-East of England. The previous day's journey to Blackton had taken Stoneham and Chang almost two hours. Today however, the Police helicopter, travelling as-the-crow-flies, arrived on location fifteen minutes after leaving Whitby.

As there was nowhere to land safely, the chopper circled the wide expanse of glistening water. In the front passenger seat, Mathew Sterling spoke to the pilot over the intercom.

'This is the location. Correct?'

'Yes, sir,' confirmed the pilot. 'This is definitely the location.'

Sterling scanned the area with high-powered binoculars. The landscape and huge man-made lake looked like any other vista in the north of England, beautiful, picturesque and benign. But, since Stoneham's visit the previous day, the vast body of water had become anything but benign.

'Okay,' said Sterling, 'let's get back to London.'

'Yes, sir.'

The helicopter banked to the south. 'Can you patch me through to my office in Vauxhall Cross, please?' said Mathew.

'Of course, sir.' said the pilot.

A few seconds later Sterling heard his secretary's voice crackle over the radio.

'Hello, sir?'

'Hello, Victoria. Please transfer me through to the Director General. This is an Alpha-One priority.'

'Right away, sir.'

Several seconds passed, with nothing but static on the line, then Sterling heard his boss's voice.

'Can you hear me, Mathew?'

'Yes, ma'am. Good afternoon.'

'Go ahead, Mathew.' said the DG, impatiently.

'We have an Alpha-One situation in the North-East, ma'am. I'm sending the location co-ordinates to you as we speak. We need to secure the whole area.'

'Understood. Go on, Mathew.'

'We need police and HAZMAT teams to the area right away.'

There was a few moments silence on the radio . . . and then.

'I've opened up those co-ordinates on my computer,' said the DG, 'we're going to need a lot more resources than just local police.'

'I agree ma'am. I suggest we contact the military at Alanbrooke Barracks. They're only an hour or so away from the location.'

'Right. I'm onto that now, Mathew. Anything else?'

'The water utilities company, ma'am. The system must be isolated immediately.'

'Yes of course. That will be my first call, Mathew.'

'Okay, thank you, ma'am. I'll see you when I get back.'

'Well done, Mathew. Well done.'

Jack leaned forward and tapped his brother on the shoulder. Mathew turned and smiled at the thumbs up sign Jack gave him.

It was almost five o'clock when the police chopper touched down on the roof of the Vauxhall Cross building. Before disembarking, Sterling leaned across and shook the pilot's hand. The three men climbed out and cleared the helideck area, then watched as the clattering aircraft lifted off.

'What now?' said Ryan Lafferty.

'I'm going to meet with the DG. And you guys are coming with me,' said Sterling.

Jack had said almost nothing during the flight back to London, and not just because of the difficulty in talking in the noisy aircraft.

'I'll catch you up,' said Jack, 'I need to make a call.'

Mathew nodded, then he and Lafferty headed for the roof access.

Jack had the smartphone to his ear as he waited for the connection. Several seconds later the familiar voice of his father-in-law, Dimitri Mikhailovich Orlov, answered.

'Jack my boy. How are you? How are Nicole and my beautiful granddaughters?'

'Dimitri. Hello. I'm fine, sir. We're all well. Where are you at the moment?'

'I'm home on the island, Jack. Why? What's the problem?'

'Nothing just yet. But I want to get Nikki and the girls down to stay with you for a little while. Is that okay?'

'Of course, my boy. I'd love to have them down here.'

'Could you send the jet, Mitri? I'd need to get them down there as soon as possible'

'Of course, Jack, of course. But what aren't you telling me?'

'Not over an open line, sir. How soon can the plane be here?'

'Give me a few minutes, Jack. I'll message you the flight details.'

'Okay. Thank you, Mitri.'

Chapter Nineteen
'Cryptosporidium'

The whiff of new paint in the Director General's office was still evident, and the summer breeze coming in through the open windows did little to dissipate the smell. As he entered her office, Jack's expression was noticed by the DG.

'Sorry about the odour gentlemen.' She gestured to the two big Chesterfields. 'Please. Let's all have a seat, she said.'

'Thank you, ma'am,' said Sterling.

The other man in the room stood and shook hands with Sterling. 'Hello, Mathew, good to see you again, old chap.'

'Anthony, hello. Yes, you too. Shame it's always when something shit happens. Oh, sorry, ma'am. Excuse me.'

'Not at all, Mathew,' said the DG, a stern look on her face. 'The situation is indeed shit.'

She turned to Castle. 'Have you met Sir Anthony Sykes, Jack?'

'No, ma'am.'

'As Jack shook hands, the DG said, 'Anthony, This is Jack Castle. Jack has helped us on a couple of occasions.'

The Masonic handshake was firm. 'My pleasure,' said Sykes.

'Anthony here is head of MI5,' she said.

Jack smiled slightly and reciprocated the secret grip. 'Pleased to meet you, Sir Anthony.'

'Just Anthony,' said Sykes, returning the smile.

'And this is another valuable member of our team, Ryan Lafferty,' said the DG.

The Irishman shook hands and they all sat down.

The Director General was the last to be seated. 'I've just come from a COBRA meeting at number 10,' she said. 'The Prime Minister has assured us she will bring all resources to bear, to ensure our people are safe. The issue of course is the virus will most likely have been in the system for at least twenty-four hours.'

'But the system is shut down now.' said Lafferty.

'Indeed,' said the DG, 'but we must assume the water supply is contaminated and respond accordingly. The police and military have secured the area and the HAZMAT team is on site. The utilities company has declared a local emergency and have issued warnings to the local population.'

'They won't be advising the locals of the real issue, I'm sure,' said Jack. 'That'd cause widespread panic. So what's their cover story, ma'am.?'

'They've announced there's been a cryptosporidium infection. All relevant instructions are being sent out via the media.'

'That's all well and good ma'am,' said Sterling, 'but, according to the briefing Ryan had from Stoneham, the virus is not just in the water. Infecting the water is only the first stage. Once infected water is consumed, the virus is passed from person to person, and will do so unchecked until . . .'

'Until we get the antidote,' interrupted Jack.

'Exactly,' said the DG. 'And as this is a domestic situation, Anthony's department will take over the UK operation. And you, Mathew, along with your very capable team, will find the antidote.'

Chapter Twenty
'Rather You Than Me, Sir'

The meeting with the Director General and Sir Anthony Sykes had gone on far longer than Jack wanted. He was keen to get back to his family and get them out of the country as soon as possible.

Back in Mathew's office, Jack said, 'I need to get home, Matt. And I don't mean in two hours on the bloody tube and train.'

'Yes, of course. I'll get a car for you.'

'Err . . . I don't think so,' said Castle. 'This time of the evening it'll take just as long to get out of the city. Can I use Victoria?'

Sterling smiled and nodded. 'Sure. I'll get her in.'

Lafferty looked puzzled, as Sterling pressed the intercom. 'Victoria, would you come in, please?'

Victoria came in. 'Yes, sir?'

'You on the bike today, Victoria?'

The girl gave a cheeky smile. 'Everyday, sir.'

'How would you like a ride out to Berkshire?'

'My pleasure, sir.' Then turning to Jack, said, 'When would you like to leave, sir?'

'Right away, if that's okay with you?' said Jack.

Her boss nodded his approval.

'I'll get changed and see you in the underground parking in ten minutes, sir.'

Ten minutes later, Jack came out of the underground carpark lift. He nodded to the tough looking security man, then waited for his brother's secretary.

He heard her before he saw her. The growl of the powerful Ducati's engine filled the space as Victoria pulled up in front of him and the security man. Jack smiled as she flipped the stand down and jumped off the big motorcycle. Jack smiled at her outfit, a skin tight red-leather biker's suite. She unclipped a spare helmet from the rear of the seat and handed it to Jack. 'We'll have you home in no time, sir.'

As she climbed back onto the bike, the security man nodded to Jack. 'Rather you than me, sir.'

Jack raised his eye-brows, and pulled on the helmet.

The tube and train journey back to East Monkton would have taken an hour and forty-five minutes at best, but Victoria pulled up to the big gates of Jack's home fifty minutes after leaving Vauxhall Cross. He leaned over to press the intercom, then took off his helmet and looked at the security camera. A few seconds later the gates swung open.

Victoria stopped the powerful machine at the front door, just as Nicole came out.

'Oh yes, Mr Castle,' she said, a huge grin on her face. 'Having fun with hot biker-chicks, huh?'

Victoria pulled off her helmet and smiled. 'Nice to see you again, ma'am.'

'It's Nicole, Victoria, no need for ma'am. And thank you for getting my husband home safely.'

'My pleasure,' said the secretary.

She started to pull her helmet back on, when Nicole said, 'Oh, bye-the-way, Victoria. Send me an email and I'll put you on the list for our charity event in a couple of weeks.'

The girl smiled, 'Oh, thank you, so much. That would be great.'

As they watch the bike disappear through the gates, Nicole turned to her husband and put her arms around his neck. After kissing him she leaned back in his arms. 'Okay, big-man. Now you can tell me why dad is sending the jet to pick us up.'

Chapter Twenty One
'Bye, Bye, Girls'

It was almost two in the morning when the Orel Corporation jet touched down at Heathrow.
Jack and his family, along with Svetlana, had been waiting in the VIP lounge for just over an hour. The twins were fast asleep in a double buggy and the nanny was half asleep on the seat next to them.

It hadn't taken Jack long to convince Nicole of the gravity of the situation in the north of England, and the horrendous consequences should the virus metastasize into the population. Nevertheless, she was very unhappy and extremely worried that Jack was not coming with them to her father's island. Her worry was compounded when he'd announced, against his better judgement, that he intended to help in any way possible, to secure the antidote.

The lounge was quiet at that time of the morning. Nicole and Jack sat close to each other on one of the big comfortable couches. She had her arm linked through his and her head against his shoulder. She too was half asleep, as she cuddled-in against her husband. Jack gently rested his cheek against her head. The familiar scent of her hair and perfume took him back to the first time he'd made love to her. He closed his eyes and inhaled, enjoying the moment, with the woman he loved.

A few seconds later a young man's voice disturbed them. 'Excuse me, sir, madam. We're ready for you to board your aircraft now.'

Jack opened his eyes, and said, 'Okay, thank you, son.'

Reluctantly, he eased Nicole's arm from his and stood up. He went over to the buggy and knelt down beside his two sleeping daughters. Gently he kissed each on the forehead. Nicole watched him with the children and smiled. She stood up and touched Svetlana's arm. 'Poidem, Sverta. Time to go.' She turned to Jack and put her arms around his neck. 'Talk soon, my darling. I love you.'

He held her for several seconds, looking into her beautiful face. 'I love you too, Nikki.'

The attendant picked up the hand luggage, as the nanny gently moved the buggy towards the exit.

'I'll watch from the window,' said Jack.

She touched his cheek. 'Be careful, Zaikin.'

Jack smiled, took her hand in his and kissed her fingers. 'Always,' he said.

He watched as his beloved family disappeared through the exit, then went quickly to the big windows that overlooked the hard-stand. Dimitri's sleek executive jet was parked right in front of the VIP building, its gleaming black fuselage sparkling in the bright lights, the corporate logo, an eagle's head, resplendent on the tail.

A few seconds later he saw his family walk the short distance to the aircraft. Nicole and the nanny gently picked up the twins and carefully climbed the short flight of steps into the cabin. The attendant loaded the hand luggage and one of the flight crew collapsed the buggy and placed it in the open hold.

Just before the cabin door closed, Nicole appeared and looked up to him. He pressed his open hand against the cold glass, then smiled as she blew him a kiss.

He watched as the aircraft was pushed back and the engines fired up. Slowly it pulled away from the stand, and then disappeared towards the end of the runway. He waited.

It was almost five minutes before he saw the sleek jet speed along the runway and lift off into the black night sky. 'Bye, bye, girls,' he said softly.

Chapter Twenty Two
'Bacon Sandwiches'

It was almost four in the morning when Jack got back home. He was not surprised to find Brian opening the front door, as he pulled the Range Rover up to the house.

'Family get away okay, boss?'

Jack nodded. 'Yeah. And now I need some sleep. So d'you, buddy.'

Brian nodded. 'I'm off t'bed now, boss. House is secure, so you should go straight up.'

'I will. Thanks, Brian. Night.'

'Morning, more like.'

Jack grinned. 'Yeah.'

The sound of Jack's smartphone woke him a few minutes after eight.

'Hello?' he said sleepily.

'Jack? Sorry to wake you. Late night?'

'It's okay, Matt. Yeah, was a long day yesterday. Didn't get to bed 'til after four. Whatsup?'

'We got another fix on Stoneham's satphone, Jack.'

Still half asleep, he sat up in bed. 'And?'

'GCHQ's had a team listening around the clock. Doing nothing but wait for it to show up again.'

'Yeah, okay,' said Jack

'They can't listen in on the conversation, but can identify when and where that phone is used.'

'Yes, I know, Matt. Get to the punch line, bro.'

Mathew sensed his brother's irritation. 'Yes, sorry, Jack. Amsterdam. The phone was used in Amsterdam.'

'And the call's destination?'

'North Korea, again. Pyongyang,' said Mathew.

The line was silent for several seconds . . . then Jack said, 'I'll see you in a couple of hours, Matt.'

'Okay, Jack. See you later.'

Being Saturday, the train from East Monkton was commuter-free and, without the hassle of the work-to-rule, the train pulled into London on time.

Along the river from Vauxhall Cross, Big Ben chimed eleven, just as Jack arrived at his brother's office. Mathew was talking on the phone as Jack entered. Jack raised his hand and nodded, then took a seat on the couch by the window. Several minutes later Mathew ended the call, flipped the intercom and said, 'Victoria, could you bring us some tea, please?'

Jack interrupted. 'Any chance of a sandwich. I haven't eaten since yesterday morning.'

Mathew nodded and continued, 'And could you get the restaurant to rustle up a couple of bacon sandwiches, please?'

Jack said, 'So what d'you think the Koreans are up too?'

Mathew looked worried. 'Not sure at the moment. But they certainly seem to be involved in some way.'

Jack shook his head slightly. 'Surely the NK government wouldn't be stupid enough to stage something like this?'

'Who the hell knows?' said Mathew, 'but just because the calls are going to Pyongyang doesn't necessarily mean it's the government.'

'Really?' said Jack, a hint of sarcasm in his voice.

'The thing is, this isn't just terrorism. If the Koreans are behind this our government may consider it an act of war. The Americans certainly will, and god-knows where it could end.'

'Christ, we need to stop this guy and get hold of the bloody antidote,' said Jack.

Mathew smiled for the first time that morning. 'Bit of an obvious statement there, Jack. But you're right.'

The knock on the door was met with the usual, 'Come,' from Mathew.

Victoria entered with a large tray, she came over and placed it on the table between the couches.

Jack smiled. 'Thanks, Victoria. That's great.'

She returned the smile. 'My pleasure,' then turning to her boss, said, 'anything else, sir?'

'No, that's fine thank you.'

As Mathew poured the tea, Jack lifted the cloche and helped himself to one of the hot bacon sandwiches. Biting into it, he said, 'Mmmm, Oh, that's bloody lovely.' He swallowed the mouthful, and continued. 'The harbour master in Whitby?'

'Andy Morgan,' said Mathew.

'Hmm,' nodded Jack, as he washed another mouthful of sandwich down with tea. 'Have you got the documents he gave you?'

Mathew went to his desk and returned with a thin folder. 'There's not much, as his office was wrecked the night before Stoneham arrived.'

'Yeah I know, but look at this,' said Jack, 'old Andy was sharp enough to photograph the passports on his phone. We know Stoneham of course, and we have pics of these other jokers, who were supposed to be ship's crew.'

'Yes,' said Mathew.

'We also have a picture of the Asian woman. The harbour master said she looked Chinese, or something.'

'Or, Korean?' said Mathew.

Jack held up the sheet of paper and pointed to the passport photo, 'Do you know who she is?'

'We know she's the woman Lilly, who Ryan met in the Russian safe house.'

'Yes, I'm sure she's Lilly. But do we know exactly who the hell she is?' said Jack.

'We're running the photograph through our terrorist data base, but nothings come up yet.'

Jack nodded. 'Okay,' then took out his phone.

It took several seconds for the call to be answered. The voice on the other end was husky with sleep. 'Hello, handsome.'

'Did I wake you, Lisa?' said Jack.

'You did, but its fine. I should be up. How you doin, honey? How's the family?'

'We're all good, babe. Listen, I'm going to send you a photograph. Could you see if you can run it through your database? See if you can get a hit?'

'No small talk then, Mr Castle? Just straight to business.'

'Sorry, Lisa, but this is really important.'

'Just kiddin, Jack. But why can't you guys run it?'

'They're trying here, but nothing is coming up at the moment.'

He heard her yawn and then. 'Oh, sorry, bit of a late night. Right, send me the pic and I'll get back to you as soon as I can.'

'Thanks, babe, you're a star,' said Jack.

'Yeah, yeah, yeah. Anything for you, darling.'

The line went silent.

Jack looked at the time on his phone. 'It's half-six in Washington. Gonna take her a while to get ready and into the office. Another couple of hours to run the mug-shot. Hopefully we should get something back late afternoon.'

Mathew nodded and said, 'How was the lovely Miss Reynard?'

Jack grinned. 'Sounded tired, and not too happy about being woken up.'

Born in New York and now almost forty, Lisa Reynard had spent most of her working life in journalism. She was now a successful and respected photo-journalist and war correspondent for the Washington Post.

She'd met Jack Castle in Baghdad in 2003 and they'd become great friends. In 2008 they'd worked together on the Iraq operation to recover a vast quantity of looted diamonds; an extra ordinarily successful mission that made them, and the rest of the team, multi-millionaires.

The last few years had seen Jack and Lisa work together on a couple of assignments, none of which had anything to do with journalism, as Lisa Reynard was also an agent for the NSA, the America National Security Agency.

Earlier in the day, Mathew had been summoned to a meeting with the Director General and the Foreign Secretary. It was now mid-afternoon and Jack was half asleep in Mathew's office, when his smartphone beeped. The time display read 15:32. He swiped the screen and said, 'Lisa?'

'Jack, hi,' unlike the morning, her voice was crisp, alert and business-like.

'What you got, babe?'

'I'm sending you a couple of shots of your mystery woman. You should get them any second.'

'Right, thanks.' His smartphone pinged and he opened the file, then scrolled through the pictures. Putting the phone back to his ear, he said, 'She's military.'

'Oh, she's more than military, Jack.'

'Yeah?'

'You're looking at Colonel Hana Chang . . . And her father is General Chang, head of North Korea's State Security.'

Chapter Twenty Three
'Cheeky Bugger'

GOVERNMENT COVERS UP TERRORIST ATTACK, said The Mail on Sunday.

NORTH EAST RESERVOIR POISONED, said The Sunday Express.

DEADLY VIRUS IN WATER SUPPLY, said the Guardian.

Jack had just finished talking to Nicole when his smartphone beeped. 'Hello, Matt.'

'Jack, good morning. I suppose you've seen today's papers?'

'Yeah,' said Jack, 'it's all over the media. Obviously been a bloody leak.'

'It was bound to happen, I suppose,' said Mathew, 'with all the military and HAZMAT up there.'

'Yeah, but the utilities company put out a pretty credible cover story. Someone else has been talking to the media.'

'Yes, of course,' said Mathew, 'but that's not the worst of it, Jack. We're now getting reports of widespread illness in the north east.'

'Widespread?' said Jack.

'Mostly Middlesbrough, which is the main area Blackton Reservoir serves. Initial reports say scores of children and older people have succumbed to asthmatic attacks.

'So it's started.'

'Yes. There are major isolation centres being set up as we speak. Anyone believed to be infected will be confined and treated as best we can. We need the antidote, Jack.'

The line was silent for several seconds . . . Jack?' said Mathew.

'Sorry, bro. Yeah I'm here, just thinking. Go ahead.'

'Okay, on a more positive note, we've had a significant breakthrough. After we picked up the sat-phone in Amsterdam, we sent Stoneham and Chang's photo's to Interpol. They've been checking all CCTV footage at airports and ports since the call. They got a hit on a Mr and Mrs Samuel Healy, flying out of Schiphol.'

'That's great. Where're they headed?'

'That's the thing, Jack. Based on Ryan Lafferty's intel, we expected Stoneham to head for Saudi.'

'So where the hell are they going?'

'They boarded a Turkish Airlines flight to Somalia.'

'Mogadishu?'

'That's right, Jack. Thing is, I can't see what they would hope to gain by releasing the virus there.'

'Nothing at all. But they could easily get into Saudi from Somali.'

'So you really think Mecca is the target?' said Mathew.

'Ryan's intel points to it,' said Jack. 'And the Haj is on right now. A million people all in one place. The virus would be devastating . . . Can you bring up a map of the Red Sea area, Matt.'

'Okay, just a second . . . right, got it. What you thinking, Jack?'

'Look at Mecca, its only sixty-odd miles from the coast. If I were planning this I'd use Somali pirates. Sail up the Red Sea. Anchor offshore. A small boat to the coast. Then an hour's drive inland. I could be in the city and back in not much more than two hours. Back on the boat, and away before anyone knew I was even on the beach.'

'Jesus, Jack, it can't be that easy,' said Mathew.

Mathew heard a chuckle on the other end of the line 'No offence little brother,' said Jack. 'But I think you've been behind that desk too long. Of course it's that easy. If you have the right network, that is.'

'Cheeky, bugger,' said Mathew.

'Yeah, sorry,' said Jack, 'when did they leave Schiphol?'

'Yesterday, but the flight was delayed over four hours. Took off at fourteen-hundred and landed early hours of the morning.'

Again there was silence on the line . . . 'Jack?'

'Okay, good. So they're gonna have to hook up with whoever Stoneham's contact is in Mogadishu. Then make the voyage up the Red Sea. All that's gonna take time. There's a pretty good chance we could catch up with them before they get to Mecca.'

'Really, Jack?' said Mathew. 'It's all a bit of a gamble isn't it?'

'Of course it is. But does the British Secret Service have any better ideas?'

This time there was silence on Mathew's end of the line . . . 'Matt?'

'Okay, Jack. What's your plan?'

'How soon can you get me a flight to Jeddah?'

Chapter Twenty Four
'Lev Zoltan'

After escaping from a UN Military Jail in Sarajevo, Dushan Grasic had been a wanted man for almost fourteen years. Staying out of prison and on the run was expensive, even in his modest hideaway in Thailand and, as his ill-gotten gains ran out, he was compelled to resume his chosen profession of mercenary and hired killer.

Grasic had worked for various terrorist organisations of every religious and political denomination. His moral compass was non-existent. His motivation was that of a true psychopath, and the Balkan War had fed his psychotic needs to murder and kill without compunction.

He'd already undertaken a couple of assignments for Gregory Stoneham, for which he'd been paid handsomely, but this mission was on a totally different scale. To infect a major city's water supply with a deadly virus and be paid two million dollars was beyond Grasic's wildest and sickest dreams.

As agreed, Stoneham had deposited a quarter of a million into Grasic's Honduran bank account, a further quarter million would be transferred once the virus was released, and on the first signs of the epidemic manifesting, the remainder of his two million would be paid.

Before leaving the Russian safe-house, Grasic had been issued with a dozen of the Baghdad virus lozenges and inoculated with the antidote. Stoneham had provided a cloned American Express credit card and fake, but credible, Bosnian passport in the name of Lev Zoltan, which would allow him to travel. But there had been no discussion on his method of entry into the United States.

'You know your business my, friend,' Stoneham had said. 'How you get into the good old US-of-A is up to you.'

After leaving the safe-house, Grasic and the Irishman, Sean Maguire, had travelled back to Moscow with the junkie-looking driver. Neither knew of each other's mission, nor did they speak about what they had been contracted to do. They'd parted company in the city and that was the last they saw of each other.

Grasic had checked into a mediocre city hotel and after picking up one of the many hookers from the bar, had spent a debauched night with the obliging and enthusiastic prostitute.

The following morning he took a cab from the city out to Sherymetovo, Moscow's main airport. As usual, Immigration Control in and out of Russia was a cluster-fuck and today was no exception. The harassed official flicked through his fake passport, gave a cursory glance at the big Bosnian's face, then stamped and handed the document back, with a curt, 'Dasvidanya.'

Two hours later Grasic took his seat in the Business Class cabin of Aeroflot flight CU89 to Havana.

Almost twelve hours later the plane touched down at Jose Marti International. Grasic was tired and annoyed the trip had not gone as he'd hoped. Although Business

Class did have better food and service, the facilities were not that great. The cocaine-fueled fuck-fest with the Moscow hooker had left him exhausted and his intention had been to sleep all the way to Cuba. Unfortunately his plan had been scuppered by the group of noisy, exuberant Russian business men, further down the cabin. On more than one occasion he'd had to restrain himself from going down and smashing them in the face.

His passage through Immigration Control was easy and, with only a rucksack, Customs formalities were just as swift. Grasic had booked a Meet-and-Greet service, like any other tourist and, as he gently pushed his way out of the Arrivals Hall, he quickly scanned the waiting throng of Cubans. A sheet of card with the printed name, Lev Zoltan, was being held aloft by a smartly uniformed young woman.

Without drawing attention to himself he eased his way to the woman. 'I'm Zoltan,' he said quietly.

'Welcome to Cuba, sir,' she said. 'May I take your bag?'

Grasic shook his head. 'No it's fine. Let's get out of here.'

The woman smiled. 'Yes, sir. The car is this way.'

It took a little over half an hour to drive from the Airport to the Marina Hemmingway. On arrival at the marina, Grasic paid the driver in American dollars. The addition of a modest tip brought a smile and a 'Thank you, sir,' from the woman.

She would not remember him as a big tipper. She would not remember him as a tourist who hit on her, as they usually did. She would not remember him as anything other than a fare to be taken from A to B and forgotten, which was exactly what Grasic wanted.

He waited until the big old American Cadillac had disappeared out of sight and then entered the main gates of the marina. Grasic nodded confidently to the old man in the gate-house, then took out his smartphone and checked the note he'd made. *South Jetty, Berth Eleven.*

The temperature was almost 40 Celsius and the six or seven minute walk to the berth took its toll. By the time he arrived at the boat, his breathing was heavy, his sodden shirt clung to his back, and the sweat ran down his face.

Grasic smiled slightly at the ornately scripted name on the stern of the craft, *Che,* and then walked across the short gangway onto the highly polished deck. 'Hello?'

A few seconds later a very tanned and fit looking young man came out from the saloon. 'Mr Zoltan?'

Grasic offered his hand and smiled, 'Yes, Lev Zoltan.'

'Hi. I'm Pablo. Welcome to Havana, sir. And welcome aboard the *Che*.'

Chapter Twenty Five
'The Coastguard'

The temperature dropped considerably once out into the Florida Straight. The sea was relatively calm and the *Che* made good headway on its voyage north towards Miami. The swell, although calm, was still enough to make Grasic queasy and, as he was still exhausted from the flight, decided to go below and sleep.

He had no idea how long he'd been out, but the change in engine noise and the slowing of the boat woke him. He went up on deck and found Pablo at the wheel. 'Are we there?' he asked.

'Not yet, sir. About another hour.'

'Why are we slowing down then?'

Pablo pointed to a fast moving ship about a half a mile away. 'We are now in American waters, sir. That's the Coastguard. They just hailed us and want us to heave-to.'

'What the fuck for?' said Grasic angrily.

Pablo looked at his passenger, surprised at the outburst from the quietly spoken man.

'There's no problem, sir. It's just routine.'

Grasic regained his composure, 'Will they board us?'

'Maybe, maybe not, sir. But we have to stop.'

The Coastguard cutter eased alongside the *Che* and a uniformed officer shouted across.   'Good afternoon, Captain.'

Pablo waved and said, 'Good afternoon, sir.'

'You're out of Havana, Captain?'

'That's correct, sir. Heading for Miami.'

'Passengers?' shouted the officer.

'Just one, sir.'

Grasic showed himself on the deck, astern of the wheelhouse, smiled and waved. 'Good afternoon.'

The officer raised his hand slightly in acknowledgement. 'Good afternoon, Mr?'

'Zoltan, Lev Zoltan. I'm just going up to Miami for the night and then back to Havana tomorrow.'

'One moment please, sir,' said the officer as he went back into the cutter's wheelhouse.

Grasic turned to Pablo and said quietly, 'What's happening?'

'Probably just checking something, sir. Don't worry.'

Grasic eyes narrowed and he grunted slightly, then put on the big smile again as the officer re-appeared.

'Okay, Captain. You can proceed with your voyage. Have a nice day, gentlemen.'

Pablo waved and shouted, 'Thank you, sir.'

The cutter eased slowly away from the *Che,* and the two men watched as the sleek craft sailed away to the south.

Grasic let out a deep breath, causing Pablo to turn and say, 'You okay, sir?'

'Yes, yes of course.' The quiet voice was back. 'I just didn't want to be held up, that's all.'

Grasic lost his balance slightly as Pablo pushed the twin throttles forward and the *Che* picked up speed. The young Cuban smiled. 'We'll be docking in Miami in about an hour, sir. Right on schedule.'

Grasic nodded and moved to the stern. He watched the Coastguard cutter getting smaller and smaller as it continued its patrol, then said quietly, 'Fucking Americans.'

Chapter Twenty Six
'General Kamal'

The General Intelligence Directorate is Saudi Arabia's national security service. After it became clear it was Saudi nationals who'd attacked the World Trade Centre, there was a huge re-shuffle of the Kingdom's security agency.

Born into a semi-noble family, Kamal bin Usef had been educated at Eton and Oxford. A further three years at Sandhurst stood him in good stead to join the Saudi Military, on his return home to Riyadh. After serving twenty five years in the army and rising to the rank of general, it was Kamal bin Usef who was now in charge of all security matters in The Kingdom of Saudi Arabia.

In the MI6 building, Mathew Sterling sat across from the Director General and listened to the secure telephone conversation between her and Kamal bin Usef. She comprehensively outlined the threat Stoneham presented and gave General Kamal all assurances that the British Government and its Security Services would support his country in any way required. The conversation ended with the usual pleasantries and the promise of all relevant documentation to follow.

Mathew saw the strain on his boss's face. 'How was he ma'am?'

'Enigmatic as ever,' said the DG. 'But he's one of Britain's strongest allies in the Middle East, and I think he loves this country as much as his own.'

'Always good to have someone like him on-side,' said Sterling. Okay, ma'am we need to move.'

'Of course, Mathew. Yes, the general has given the green light. Let's get our team to Jeddah with all haste. Jack will be met by General Kamal's best men on his arrival.'

'Not sure that will sit too well with Jack, ma'am. He's always been the one to run his own show.'

The DG's infrequent smile appeared. 'Yes indeed. Jack is somewhat of a maverick, but I'm confident he's smart enough to manage the situation.'

'Indeed,' said Sterling. 'If you'll excuse ma'am.'

'Yes. Thank you, Mathew. Keep me informed. I'm off to number 10 now to update the Prime Minister '

Sterling nodded and stood up. 'Ma'am.'

As he was leaving the room the DG said, 'Mathew.'

Sterling turned. 'Ma'am?'

'Tell your brother to be safe.'

As Mathew rode the lift back down to his office he thought about her last comment, a wry smile on his face. Little did she know, Jack was already on his way to Jeddah.

Chapter Twenty Seven
'I Gotta Get One Of These'

Time was critical and the situation in the north of England was escalating, with many more of the local population showing first signs of the infection. Those already infected had not yet slipped into the pneumonic stage and, according to the information provided by Ryan Lafferty, the final stages would not manifest for seven to ten days. This meant the antidote had to be secured in the next week. The isolation units were taking in more infected victims each day and all that could be done, was to administer antibiotics . . . and pray.

Porton Down is the UK's Science and Technology Laboratory and operated exclusively for the Ministry of Defence. The site itself may not be top secret, but the work that goes on there most certainly is. Its key role is to research and develop defence systems against chemical and biological attacks. The best microbiologists in the country had been working around the clock since the infection of Blackton Reservoir was discovered. The general consensus was an antidote for the Baghdad virus could be produced, but it would take several months to finesse a pathogen strong enough to combat the virus. With little more than a week before the final stages of the infection took hold, the only way to stop thousands of people dying was to secure the antidote.

The Royal Air Force Tornado, after travelling at almost a thousand miles an hour, touched down at Jeddah International Airport four hours after leaving RAF Brize Norton. The two-seater fighter aircraft, being faster by far than any commercial or private jet available, had been secured by Mathew for Jack's flight to Saudi Arabia.

The sleek aircraft came to a stand-still at a remote site away from the main terminal. Two Saudi Military vehicles waited as the jet's engines wound down and fell silent. The Perspex canopy hissed open and Jack eased himself out of the rear seat. Before climbing down the side of the aircraft, he shook hands with the pilot. 'That was the most amazing flight I've ever had. Thank you, Wing Commander. I really gotta get one of these.'

The young flight officer smiled. 'You're welcome, sir. And if you want one it will only cost you thirty five million.'

Jack grinned. 'Yeah, well, maybe not. Have a safe flight back, Commander.'

The pilot gave a casual salute. 'Good luck, sir.'

As Jack walked towards the waiting vehicles an officer stepped forward. 'Mr Castle, sir?'

'Yes, Major. I'm Jack Castle.'

'I'm Major Ibrahim Masood. General Kamal sends his compliments, sir.'

'Thank you, Major.'

Once in the vehicle, Masood offered Jack a bottle of water, then said, 'We have stationed patrols all along the coast and . . .'

Jack interrupted. 'Excuse me, Major. That's not good. If Stoneham even smells a patrol he'll disappear. Right now he doesn't know we're onto him. This mission is not just about stopping them infecting your people. It's about securing the antidote, and the only way to do that is capture Stoneham.'

The officer looked shocked at being told what to do. 'But we must protect . . .'

'I'm sorry, Major,' said Jack. 'The man we're dealing with is a very capable and deadly individual. If he sees any sign of military or security, he'll just vanish. But I understand your position. Have your patrols dress in civilian clothes. No use of military vehicles. Low profile. Okay?'

The officer's dark eyes narrowed and a slight smile appeared. As the vehicles drove away the major spoke into the radio. Jack's Arabic was basic, but good enough to understand what was being said. He looked at the officer and smiled. 'Thank you, sir. Now how fast can we get to Mecca?'

Chapter Twenty Eight
'Why?'

The *Che* was about a mile from the mouth of the Miami Beach Marina, when Pablo shouted, 'We'll be entering the harbour in a few minutes, sir.'

Below deck, in the main cabin, Grasic heard the young Cuban's call. He took the speargun from the wall and carefully loaded the arrow-like harpoon into the shaft of the gun, then pulled back the strong elastic and hooked it onto the firing mechanism. Before leaving the cabin he picked up a broad-bladed diver's knife and slipped it into his waist band.

As he quietly climbed the short flight of steps, he heard Pablo shout again, 'Sir?'

Grasic entered the wheel-house, as the Cuban turned and saw the weapon. The look on the handsome young face changed from surprise to shock, as the deadly harpoon thumped into his body.

With an agonising scream he was thrown back against the bulkhead. Grabbing at his chest, and his face wracked with pain, he slumped slowly to the polished wooden deck.

The *Che* lurched with the wheel unattended; Grasic slowly moved across the cabin and steadied the boat.

'Why?' said Pablo weakly. A stream of blood bubbled from his open mouth.

Grasic looked ahead and, as he spun the wheel to starboard, the boat changed direction and sailed past the entrance to the marina.

Pablo, in the last throes of death, tried to move, the hideous looking spear protruding from the centre of his chest. 'You . . . bastard,' he said, as he grabbed his killer's leg.

Grasic turned and viciously kicked the dying man away, then slowly drew the big diver's knife from his waistband.

The Bay Harbour Islands are only a couple of miles north from the Miami Marina. Many of these islands are privately owned, others have several large villas or a collection of smaller houses. A further three miles past the Islands, is a small secluded cove with the tiniest of beaches. Grasic took the powerful binoculars and scanned the beach area. It was dusk, with a full moon rising in the evening sky. He looked at his watch. In half an hour the beach area would be in almost total darkness. He pointed the bow of the *Che* into the oncoming current and dropped the forward anchor. The boat rocked gently as it held-station a mile or so out from the tiny beach.

Grasic looked at the body behind him. He went down to the cabin and took off all his clothes. Coming back up, he pulled the harpoon from the dead Cuban's chest. The sucking noise, as the vicious barbed point left the man's flesh, made Grasic smirk. He threw the harpoon over the side, along with the speargun; the blood covered diver's knife went next.

Taking the man's legs, he dragged him out of the wheelhouse and up to the stern of the rocking boat. A small anchor was clipped to the stern bulkhead. Grasic unscrewed the chain and released the anchor. He unfastened the Cuban's belt and looped it through the ring on the anchor shaft. After re-fastening the belt, he eased the body of Pablo up onto the bulwark. *He's heavier than he looks*, thought the wheezing Bosnian. *But dead weight is always heavier.* He steadied himself and then, as the boat dipped with the swell, pushed the ill-fated Cuban over the stern. He watched for a few seconds as the body floated away, and then the anchor did its job, taking the young man's body to the bottom of the shark infested waters.

Grasic took up the binoculars and checked the area again. The beach was now in darkness and the cliff top deserted. The next hour was spent cleaning the deck, bulkhead and stern of the boat. He'd wiped down everywhere to remove his fingerprints and then diligently spread two gallons of bleach over everything.

After getting dressed, he checked his watch, a little after seven. He scanned the beach area again, then went up to the forward deck and carefully lowered the inflated dingy over the side. With a firm grip of the painter, he pulled the tiny craft along the side of the boat and around to the stern, then securely tied it alongside. He looked around once more then, satisfied all appeared normal, carefully scrambled into the unsteady craft. He slipped the knot holding the dingy then lost his balance slightly as the rubber boat floated away on the current. It took him several attempts to get the small outboard motor fired-up. Finally, after several outbursts of, 'Shit, Fuck, Bastard,' and, 'Fuck,' again, the small engine gurgled into life. As he turned the tiller towards the shore he looked back over his shoulder at the now abandoned *Che*.

With no wind and a very warm evening, the hundred or so steps to the clifftop took its toll on the wheezing Bosnian. Gasping for breath, he sat down on the grass and looked out to sea. The full moon shone on the black waters and the *Che*, rocking gently at anchor, could be seen clearly in the moon-light. For a second, he thought of the young Cuban . . . and then shrugged his shoulders. With his breath and heart-rate back to normal, Grasic picked up his rucksack and headed towards the outskirts of Miami.

Chapter Twenty Nine
'Archangel'

Grasic walked quickly from the clifftop into town. He hadn't expected the short walk to be so arduous, but the warm evening air and his brisk pace had caused him to sweat heavily. By the time he arrived at the Aventura Mall his shirt clung to his back and the sweat trickled down his face.

The cold air-conditioning made him shiver as he entered the big shopping centre. He took out his phone and checked the note he'd made, *Coffee King*. He went to the information display and found his current location, then that of *Coffee King*. It took several more minutes to get to the cafe, by which time the Bosnian was wheezing again and in serious need of water. He took a seat at one of the outside tables and got his breath back, just as a young waitress arrived. 'Good evening sir. What can I get you?'

Grasic gave a weak smile. 'Bottled water and black coffee, please.'

'Sure, sir. Anything to eat?' said the girl.

He shook his head, as he took out his smartphone. He found the number then quickly typed out a short text message, *Archangel,* then touched SEND.

The waitress returned and placed the drinks on the table. 'Anything else, sir?'

'No, thank you,' he said, as his phone pinged.

He swiped the screen and read the message. *40/45 minutes.*

He'd been waiting for over half an hour and had drunk a second coffee, when he saw two police officers approaching. He calmly picked up the menu, placed it on the table and, with head bowed forward, read through the list of *Exciting New Sandwiches*. From the corner of his eye he watched as the cops strolled past. He was still reading the sandwich list when the shadow of a man fell across the table. The Bosnian looked up and smiled slightly, then nodded to the other seat.

The new arrival looked around and then sat down.

The waitress returned. 'Can I get you anything, sir?'

'Bottled water, please,' said the new arrival.

The girl left and Grasic said quietly, 'Milosh, my old friend. How long has it been?'

They finished their drinks and paid the bill, leaving a small gratuity, which received a, 'Thank you, guys. Have a nice evening,' from the young waitress.

As they strolled out of the mall they said very little. Once outside Milosh said, 'The car is over here.' then continued. 'Fifteen years.'

Grasic turned to his friend. 'What?'

'You asked how long it's been. Fifteen years.'

'Ah, yes,' said Grasic. 'The outskirts of Srebrenica. The fucking UN Peace-keepers had us trapped in the village.'

'Yes. You gave me and Slovan the last working truck. You stayed and fought. You saved us.'

'Yes, my friend. But I was badly wounded and needed a hospital. Those fuckers had to take care of me.'

Milosh nodded. 'Of course. It was the smart option. But you still saved us.'

Grasic nodded. 'And yes, they took care of me . . . then threw me in prison.'

The two old comrades laughed.

On the far side of the huge carpark they approached a nondescript station wagon. 'This okay?' said Milosh.

Grasic nodded. 'Perfect.'

As Milosh clicked the doors open, three young Hispanics appeared from the nearby bushes.

'Hey, homes. Nice ride,' said the tallest of the kids.

'What?' said Milosh.

The tall kid smiled and swaggered round the car, followed by his two companions. 'Keys, homes.'

The two Bosnians looked at each other. Milosh looked at the tall one and said, 'Fuck off, grease-ball. Before you get hurt.'

The smiles on the Hispanics vanished, as each produced a switch-blade knife.

'Grease-ball?' said the tall kid. 'Aint no grease-balls here, grandpa. Now gimme the fucking keys.'

Milosh looked at the kid for several seconds, and then threw the keys at his feet. 'Okay. Okay. We don't want any trouble. It's only a car.'

The kid grinned and bent down to retrieve the keys. When he stood up, Milosh was holding a large Glock automatic. 'Typical kids these days, brings a knife to a gun-fight. Now fuck off, grease-balls.'

'Hey?' The shout came from the two police officers running towards them. The gang bolted and Milosh looked at his friend. Grasic nodded, and in a single motion Milosh turned and fired at the oncoming officers, killing the first and wounding the second.

'Let's go!' yelled Grasic.

By the time they drove onto the freeway, there were three police cars in pursuit. A police helicopter had its searchlight on the station wagon and two news choppers were following the chase, which was now being relayed live to the TV sets of North Miami.

Chapter Thirty
'Good News, Bad News'

Jack's smartphone beeped and he looked at the display. He swiped the screen and said, 'Hi, Mathew,'

Jack could hear the strain in his brother's voice. 'We have good news and bad news, Jack.'

'The good news is?' said Jack.

'The Americans have captured Dushan Grasic in Florida.'

'Normally I'd be happy to hear that, Matt. So what's the bad news?'

'The bad news is, he wasn't carrying the virus.'

'Oh, Jesus, Matt. So he's used it?'

'No, no. He had the lozenges with him, but they were fake, Jack.'

The line was quiet for several seconds . . . 'Jack?'

'Yeah, I'm here, Matt. So it's fair to say Grasic would not have been administered with the antidote either?'

'Fraid not. They tested his blood and found nothing out of the ordinary.'

Again the line went silent . . . Mathew waited . . . 'Jack? What're you thinking?'

'Fucking decoys, Matt. He's used them as decoys. Sean Maguire and Dushan Grasic were being used as decoys and carried the fake virus.'

This time the line was quiet on Mathew's end . . .
'Matt?' said Jack.

'Sorry,' said Mathew. 'So d'you think he knew Sean Maguire was an imposter? That Maguire was really Ryan Lafferty?'

'It doesn't matter if he knew or not. He was still used as a decoy, so that Stoneham and Chang could infected the Blackton Reservoir themselves.'

'And now they're on the way to the Kingdom,' said Mathew.

'Yeah. But Grasic was captured in America. Does that mean Stoneham will head for America, after Saudi?'

'Maybe. Who the hell knows? Our only hope now is to capture Stoneham in Saudi. It's up to you, Jack.'

Chapter Thirty One
'Marco Vilnius'

It was early morning at Dulles International, Washington's main airport. Five flights had arrived, all within fifteen minutes of each other, and the mass of passengers heading for Immigration Control was huge.

Marco Vilnius waited nervously as the people in front of him were herded into organised lines by the immigration staff. The Border Control officers, at the twenty or so desks, carefully scrutinised each person as they presented themselves, and their documents, for entry into the United States. Marco was surprised how fast the passengers were being processed and, as his turn came closer, his anxiety increased.

'Next, please,' said the uniformed attendant.

Vilnius did not move.

'Sir, your next. Desk eleven, please.'

Marco smiled nervously and stepped forward. At the desk he handed over his documents and waited as the officer flicked through the new Lithuanian passport.

'First time in America, sir?'

'What?'

'This your first trip to America?'

Marco smiled again. 'Oh, yes. Sorry. Yes, first time.'

'Business or pleasure, sir?'

'What?'

'The purpose of your visit. Is it business or you here on vacation?'

'Oh, vacation. Yes.'

'Where will you be staying in Washington, sir?'

'The err . . . the Scarlet Hotel.'

The thump of the stamp on the passport made him jump slightly, then the officer handed back the documents. 'Welcome to America, sir. Have a nice day.'

After clearing Customs, Vilnius came out into the busy Arrivals Hall. Looking around he saw the signs for WASHROOMS. He quickly entered and went to the first sink. The place was busy, but no one paid him any attention. He swilled cool water onto his face and then looked at himself in the mirror. He looked good in the Hugo Boss suit and dark grey shirt. The scruffy hair was cut short and gelled and the stubbly beard gone. He now looked like any other thirty year old well-dressed businessman, not the junkie-looking driver he was three days ago.

For the first time since leaving Moscow, he smiled confidently.

Chapter Thirty Two
'The Talisman'

Greg Stoneham and Hana Chang had left St Petersburg in the seagoing vessel *Kristina*. He was happy his entry in, and exit out of the UK, had gone as planned. The virus had been introduced to the reservoir without any issues, and after making the sat-phone call to the General in Pyongyang, his next payment of two million dollars had been deposited into his Montenegro bank.

The voyage from Whitby to Holland had been reasonably comfortable. The *Kristina* coped with the heavy chop of the North Sea admirably and their entry into Amsterdam Marina passed without issue.

The next day saw Stoneham agitated, as the flight from Schiphol to Somali had been delayed several hours. The morning though had not been wasted as his meeting, with the old Jew in the Amsterdam Diamond Quarter, had gone better than expected.

'What are we doing here?' asked Lilly, when they arrived at the little shop.

'Getting our good luck charm,' he said, then pushed the button on the heavy glass security door.

A few seconds later a buzz was heard as the door opened. They stepped into a small vestibule and as the outer door closed a second buzz was heard. The inner security door clicked open. An old man greeted them as they entered the tiny shop. He offered his hand to Stoneham. 'Very good to see you again, sir.'

Stoneham nodded. 'You too, Mr Shapiro.'

'This way, please,' said the old man.

They went to the rear of the shop, climbed a short flight of stairs and entered a small workshop. The old man sat down at his bench, opened a drawer and took out a blue leather box. He laid a piece of velvet on the bench and placed the box in the centre. After putting on a pair of thick spectacles he opened the box and removed the item. Hana Chang looked on unimpressed at what the jeweller placed on the velvet.

'Very nice,' said Stoneham.

'Thank you, sir. It's always a pleasure to prepare something for you.'

Stoneham nodded, slightly. 'And your payment has gone through?'

'Yes, thank you, sir. Arrived in our account yesterday.'

Stoneham picked up the item and held the ends of the chain. 'Turn around, please,' he said to Chang.

She frowned and did as he asked, then shivered slightly as his fingers touched the back of her neck.

'There,' he said, as he looked at the pendant.

'Beautiful,' said the old Jew.

Hana Chang said nothing.

Once outside she said, 'What the hell was that all about?'

'I told you. It's our good luck charm. Our Talisman for the mission.'

'It looks cheap and frankly quite ugly.'

Stoneham looked serious. 'Do not take it off until the mission is completed.'

Chang shrugged slightly. 'I didn't have you down as a superstitious man.'

He smiled again. 'We can always use some good luck. Just don't take it off.'

Chapter Thirty Three
'Gold Teeth'

Somalia . . . another war-torn African nation, where the spectre of death hangs in the air like a Dickensian fog, and hunger is the weapon of choice for the brutal controlling warlords.

Mogadishu, on the east coast, is the epicentre of this broken nation and the Bakaara Market area, in the middle of the city, is the stronghold of the most powerful of the warlords and Somali Pirates.

Mohamed Farrah Aidid ruled this ravaged country until he was killed in 1996. Today, his younger, lesser known brother, Suleiman Farrah Aidid, controls the biggest band of pirates operating in the Indian Ocean and Red Sea region.

Stoneham's relationship with Hana Chang hadn't improved and, although there was plenty of talk about the mission, very little small-talk had transpired. Indeed, he was hoping, as they spent more time together in the role of man and wife, there might be the opportunity to enjoy some sexual encounter, but it was clear she did not like the man she'd been forced to work with.

The Turkish Airlines flight had taken almost eleven hours. It was after two in the morning when the plane touched down at Aden Adulle International, Mogadishu's main airport.

The transition through Immigration was made less laborious by the introduction of a one hundred dollar bill into each of Mr and Mrs Samuel Healy's passports. Customs procedures were dealt with in the same way, and the big shiny-black face of the Customs Officer beamed, as the carefully folded one hundred dollar bill was discreetly passed to him.

Most of the passengers on the flight had been Somalis. With only a handful of Europeans exiting the terminal, the large group of taxi drivers overwhelmed each foreigner, all touting for their business and foreign currency. The vicious snarls from Stoneham and the threat of being hit with the man's cane, did little to dissuade the drivers, until two very large black men pushed through the melee, causing the grumbling cabbies to retreat to their respective vehicles.

The larger of the two men smiled, showing a mouthful of gold teeth. 'Mr Sam-well Heeely?'

'Yes. I'm Samuel Healy, this is my wife Lilly.'

The big man leered at the beautiful Asian woman, 'Okay, this way, boss.'

The crowd parted as the two big men cleared the way to the waiting, illegally parked, 4x4. A third Somali stood by the vehicle, a large Magnum revolver ready in his hand. As Stoneham and Chang appeared, with their two escorts, the third man quickly slipped the big handgun into his shoulder holster. He nodded to the foreigners, and the stern look on his face changed to yet another golden-toothed smile.

The drive from the airport to the outskirts of the city was swift and dangerous. The driver, who appeared to be under the influence of some sort of drug, was weaving in and out of the traffic, sounding the horn and cursing the lesser mortals in his way. The two big black men grinned and chattered between themselves at the antics of the crazed driver. In the back, Stoneham and Chang hung on to their broken seat belts, as the big 4x4 cut its way along the busy streets and out towards the coast.

Fifteen minutes after leaving the terminal, the 4x4 pulled up in front of a reasonable looking beach hotel. The two big men climbed out and the larger of the two nodded towards the entrance. 'You stay here tonight, boss. In morning, Commander Aidid come see you.'

'Thank you.' said Stoneham.

The big man flashed the golden smile, leered once again at the woman, then climbed back into the 4x4. The expected squeal of tyres, as the vehicle sped away, made Stoneham smirk slightly, then turn and walk up the steps, into the poorly lit hotel foyer.

Chapter Thirty Four
'Vivid Saturation'

The rooms had been clean, if not particularly luxurious, and Stoneham had slept reasonably well. Hana Chang, on the other hand, was far less relaxed and hardly slept at all.

At breakfast the coffee was not good, nor was the food on offer at the mediocre buffet. The few pieces of fresh fruit that were available look quite edible, so they made do with that. They couldn't find any bottled water, and settled for cans of some un-known orange drink, then sat out on the front veranda to wait for Aidid.

The wind coming off the Indian Ocean cooled the morning and made it far more comfortable outside, than in the inadequately air-conditioned hotel.

It was almost eleven o'clock when Commander Suleiman Farrah Aidid turned up in a dust cloud of four trucks. Over a dozen heavily armed men jumped from three of the vehicles and set a perimeter around the fourth. As the air cleared the door was held open and Commander Aidid stepped out. Stoneham resisted the urge to smile at the pseudo military efforts made by Aidid's band of pirates. He was, however, impressed by the man himself. Tall and dressed in a pale grey linen suit with dark blue shirt, he looked as though he'd just stepped out of a fashion magazine. In his late thirties with a shaven head and tribal scars on his cheeks, Stoneham thought he looked remarkably like the singer, Seal.

Aidid joined them on the veranda and offered his hand. 'Mr Healy?'

'Commander Aidid,' said Stoneham, as they shook hands. 'And this is my wife, Lilly.'

'Of course it is,' said Aidid, knowingly. He took Chang's hand and raised it to his lips. 'A pleasure, Lilly.'

Aidid turned and waved to a small very thin Indian man, who quickly scuttled up the steps to join the group.

'So,' said Aidid. 'To business.'

They entered the foyer and the commander looked around, then pointed to a table directly under a revolving ceiling fan. 'Over here I think.'

Three of the pirates followed the group while the rest stood guard outside, the half dozen or so other guests in the foyer quickly disappeared, much to the delight of Aidid's minders.

The little Indian sat down and placed a small briefcase on the table. Stoneham, Chang and Aidid watched as he deftly flicked open the lid and took out several items, carefully placing each on the table in front of him. A small rubber mat, two pairs of fine pliers, a small digital weighing scale, a pocket calculator and a notepad.

'Ready?' said Aidid.

The Indian smiled nervously. 'Yes, Commander.'

Stoneham leaned across and said to Chang, 'Excuse me, my dear,' then reached around and unclipped the pendant from her neck.

The Indian took the jewel and held it up to the light. 'Hrrrmmm,' he said almost adoringly.

The three watched as the little man laid the pendant on the mat and began his work. The chain was clipped off, as were the half dozen tiny seed pearls. The rear setting was removed, leaving the centre piece of the pendant, a rough blue stone, about the size of a large Brazil nut. The Indian took out a clean white handkerchief and rubbed the stone, placed it on the scale, and noted the weight on his pad. He picked up the calculator and punched in some numbers, again making a note on the pad.

Hana Chang looked-on bemused, as the Indian continued his work. No one else spoke as they too were intent on the little man's efforts.

The Indian fitted a jeweller's loupe into his eye and again held the stone up to the light. Several seconds past, and then the Indian, almost reverently, laid the jewel back on the mat.

Aidid leaned forward and said, 'Well?'

'Yes, Commander,' said the man, with an air of confidence and pride. 'What we have here is an uncut Kashmiri sapphire, vivid saturation, which of course means excellent colour and clarity. Uncut weight . . .' he looked at the notepad, 'Ninety-six karats, with a value in excess of one hundred thousand dollars. And when cut, most certainly double that.'

Aidid sat back and smiled. Stoneham looked across at Hana Chang, her beautiful eyes wide and mouth open.

'Thank you, Karim,' said Aidid to the Indian. Then he leaned across and picked up the sapphire. He removed the silk handkerchief from his breast pocket, dropped in the stone and replaced the jaunty piece of attire. 'Now, Mr Healy. How may we help you?'

Chapter Thirty Five
'The Old Dhow'

The meeting at the beach hotel ended with the assurance Commander Aidid would facilitate Stoneham's covert entry in and out of The Kingdom of Saudi Arabia. He would also provide several elements to assist Stoneham on his mission.

At no time did the Somali ask 'what' that mission was or 'why' the American needed to get into the Kingdom discreetly. Nor did he really care. He did however consider simply killing Healy, and taking the sapphire along with the beautiful Lilly, but the promise, from the man with the fancy walking cane, to provide several of the new shoulder-launch missiles, was too good to miss, and the deal was done.

Two hours later, a Huey helicopter came clattering in to land on the hotel's beachfront. Stoneham grinned at the old American Military workhorse, and waited as the rotors wound down and the blinding sandstorm dissipated.

'Is that thing safe?' said Chang.

'We'll soon find out,' said the grinning Stoneham.

The side door slid open and what looked like a pilot, dressed in flying suit and helmet waved them forward.

146

The two trotted down the beach and climbed in to the old aircraft. Sitting in the pilot's seat, also in flying suit and helmet, was Commander Aidid. He removed his RayBans. 'Strap in and enjoy the flight,' he said, then put the sunglasses back on, gave a big smile, and continued, 'We'll be on the north coast in about an hour.'

Stoneham and Chang did as instructed, seating themselves across from the two big black men, who'd met them at the airport. Both of which gave their golden-toothed smiles

True to his word, and just over an hour later, Aidid expertly landed the old Huey on one of the loading docks at Berbera Harbour. The two minders jumped out first, AK47's at the ready. Mr and Mrs Healy were courteously helped down, quickly followed by the dashing Commander Aidid.

'This is one of my ships,' said the commander, pointing to an old Arab dhow.

Stoneham and Chang followed the Somali to the edge of the dock and looked at the old boat.

Aidid flashed the perfect smile and said, 'Its appearance is meant to fool you, my friend.'

'It's certainly fooling me,' said Chang, clearly unimpressed. 'It'll take a week to get up the Red Sea in that thing.'

Aidid frowned and feigned offence. Then the big smile re-appeared. 'To all intents and purposes yes, it is an old dhow. But we have made a few modifications. The interior of the hull has been reinforced with fibreglass for strength of course, but also to keep the weight down. It has satellite navigation and can identify any ship within a three hundred mile radius. If you look at the hull, just in front of the centre mast, you will see a long hatch. There is one each side of the ship. When open, we are able to run-out the automated Gatling gun cannons, the same as the Americans use on their Blackhawk helicopters. There's another mounted in the stern.' The commander smiled again and spoke as if showing off one of his prize possessions. 'But what really makes this dhow special is the twin Rolls Royce diesel engines, making this one of the fastest ships in the region.

Stoneham smiled. 'When can we set sail, Commander?'

'As soon as you board my friend.'

Two men came down the gangway and shook hands with Aidid. One of which was introduced to Stoneham. 'This is my cousin, Captain Gassim; he will see you are given all the support you require. He knows you are very special friends of mine and you will be treated as such, have no fear.'

Stoneham nodded and said, 'Thank you, Commander.'

As the two men shook hands, Aidid said, 'Have a pleasant voyage, my friend. I shall see you when you return.'

Chapter Thirty Six
'Preamonitus, Preamonitus'

Jack had not been subject to the normal immigration controls at King Abulaziz Airport. Major Masood had been given instructions to meet Mr Castle and get him to Mecca with all haste.

'Takes about an hour to get to Mecca from here?' said Jack.

'Oh, we'll be there much sooner than that, sir,' said Masood.

The two jeeps skirted the long runway and arrived at the military side of the airport a few minutes after Jack had climbed out of the Tornado.

Jack smiled. 'Good,' he said, when he saw the helicopter.

General Kamal is waiting for us at the Al-Haram Mosque. We should be there in about twenty minutes, sir.'

Jack still wore the flying suit over his slacks and shirt and as the temperature was in the mid-forties he was sweating considerably. The jeeps came to a halt on the edge of the helipad. Masood's men, in single file, moved to the aircraft and climbed aboard. The colonel however waited, as his charge stripped off the flying suit and threw it into the vehicle.

'That's better,' said Jack, then picked up his bottle of water, 'Okay, let's go.'

As the helicopter clattered into the clear blue sky, Jack looked out of the window and mentally went through his knowledge of the Hajj. *Three days of prayer at the Al-Haram Mosque . . . The circumvention of the Kaaba . . . Ritual washing . . . Drinking from the Well of Zamzam . . . The stoning of the devil at the three pillars . . . The vigil at Mount Arafat . . .*

The pilot's voice broke into his thoughts. 'Landing in three minutes. Stand by.'

Jack had been so engrossed, he'd failed to see the spectacle on the ground below. The chopper was at a thousand feet and coming in to land a few hundred yards north of the fabulous Al-Haram Mosque.

The huge mosque is the central place for the Hajj pilgrims. Over the years it has been extended and grown in size and beauty. The main courtyard, in the centre of the mosque, is where the faithful undertake the ritualistic circumvention of the *Kaaba.* The silk covered, cube-like building, believed by Muslims to represent *The House of Allah.* Seven times they walk around the sacred structure and, with up to three hundred thousand devotees all dressed the same, and moving as one, it looks like a sea of white gently circling this most holy of places.

'Amazing,' said Jack, as the chopper passed over the mosque.

Colonel Masood looked out the window. 'Yes, indeed. We expect well over two million worshippers this year.'

The helicopter landed in the usual storm of sand and dust. Jack and the Colonel climbed out, swiftly followed by Masood's men. Three vehicles stood by. The heat further inland was even greater than at Jeddah and Jack was feeling decidedly dehydrated, *I'm getting too old for this shit,* he thought. He looked at Masood, not a sweat stain anyway, *yeah, definitely getting too old.* They quickly boarded the 4x4's, 'Thank God for that,' said Jack, without realising.

'Sir?' said Masood.

Jack grinned. 'Oh, sorry, Colonel. Just thankful for the air-con.'

'Ah,' smiled the soldier. 'But I thought you had spent a lot of time in the Middle East, sir?'

Jack nodded, 'I have, but I'm not usually running around like you guys do. Well, not much anyway.'

The colonel smiled and said nothing. They pulled up at a large modern building that looked like some swish corporate offices.

'Right, sir. Here we are.'

As he climbed out, Jack said, 'And this is?'

'This is the main security building for the Al-Haram Mosque. This way please, sir.'

As they entered the splendid foyer a security officer approached, then stood aside and snapped a salute when he recognised Colonel Masood.

A few minutes later they entered a large outer office, where two female officers were working at their desks. The older of the two stood as Jack and the colonel entered.

'Good afternoon, Colonel,' she said, then turning to Jack, 'Good afternoon, sir. This way please.'

At the order to 'Come in,' she opened the ornate door and stood to one side as the two men entered.

'Colonel Masood, General,' said the woman.

'Thank you, Lieutenant.'

The colonel stood to attention and presented a very smart salute. The general casually reciprocated. 'Thank you, Colonel,' then approached Jack and offered his hand. 'Mr Castle. A great pleasure to meet you. I've heard many good things about you, my dear.'

Jack smiled at the general's comment, knowing that the use of, *My Dear,* in the Muslim world, was only for the closest of friends.

'Thank you, General. Please call me Jack, sir.'

'Of course . . . Jack. Indeed it is good to meet you. I only wish it were in more harmonious circumstances.'

'Me too, sir. Me too.'

'Right let's all have a seat and something to drink.'

'I'm not sure where anything is here,' said the general, smiling, 'this is not my office. Our Chief of Security for the mosque has been moved next door.' Jack nodded and smiled.

'I don't think he was too happy about it, but needs must,' continued the general, 'Colonel, could you ask one of the officers to bring us some water and juices please? Jack do you need anything to eat. I'm sure you're exhausted after you flight?'

'I'm good, sir. Just water please.'

With drinks passed around and the three men seated, General Kamal began, 'I have received several documents from your Director General, Jack. As always the British security service is most co-operative.'

Jack nodded and smiled slightly, anxious to get a plan formulated. 'Stoneham is an extremely dangerous individual, sir, with a network of assets that almost matches our own. As you know, he's already managed to infect a major water facility in the north of England.'

'Yes, Jack, he is indeed a specialist of his craft,' said Kamal, 'but I believe we are a match for him, my dear. And to be honest, we don't really know if he intends to attack the Kingdom, do we?'

Jack took a large drink of water. 'We've been able to track him each time he uses his sat-phone, sir. We know he left Amsterdam for Mogadishu. We believe he has contacts in Somalia. We also believe there would be no significant benefit in an attack on Somalia. The Kingdom is the prime target, sir. Especially with the Hajj in full swing.'

'Yes of course, we must be prepared, and I've always believed in the old English proverb *preamonitus, preamonitus,'* said the general.

Jack frowned slightly. 'Sorry, sir, but my Latin is a little rusty.'

'Excuse me, Jack. The product of an English education, my dear. *Preamonitus, preamonitus.* Forewarned is forearmed.'

Jack nodded. 'Absolutely, sir.'

General Kamal looked at the two men in front of him. 'Now, gentlemen, let's decide how we are going to stop our rogue American friend.'

Chapter Thirty Seven
'Dog Walkers & Joggers'

The McMillan Reservoir is the main source of Washington DC's water supply and is situated in the Bloomingdale area, between the Potomac and Anacostia rivers. The Howard University borders the west shoreline of this large manmade lake and the surrounding parkland is a popular place for walks and relaxation by students and city residents alike.

Marco Vilnius had left Dulles Airport and, although informing the Immigration Officer of his intended place of residence, The Scarlet Hotel was the last place he intended to go. It was just before dawn when the taxi dropped him off at the junction of 5th Street and McMillan Drive, within the grounds of the university.

At this time of the morning there were few people around, a couple of dog-walkers, three of four joggers and the odd street cleaner. None of them paid any attention to the smartly dressed man, walking towards the edge of the picturesque body of water.

Vilnius found a bench under an old Acacia tree and sat down. He placed his briefcase on the seat next to him. For a second he was startled as a young woman jogged past. He waited until she was gone and then carefully spun the tumblers on the case. The innocuous contents, gave nothing away, some underwear, a shirt, a toilet bag and a small box of branded antacid lozenges. In the lid-flap were a couple of pairs of rubber surgical gloves.

Once again he looked around, a dog walker fifty yards away was busy picking up the deposit his animal had just left; a couple of young men jogging on the far side of the reservoir; a lone rower sculling swiftly up the long expanse of water.

Vilnius carefully pulled on the rubber gloves, smoothing them snugly over his fingers. He took out the box of antacid lozenges and put them in his jacket pocket, then closed the lid on the case. He walked casually to the edge of the water and checked around one more time. The dog walker had gone and the rower was now a good three hundred yards away. He was alone. He put the case on the ground and took the box from his pocket. He carefully unwrapped, and tossed each lozenge into the water, watching as each floated and then dissolved.

As he walked away he dropped the wrappings, the box and gloves, into a nearby waste bin. Another jogger came bounding around a large clump of bushes, startling him again, then carried on up the side of the lake. Vilnius took a deep breath and carried on walking.

It took a little over ten minutes to exit the university grounds and out onto Georgia Avenue. There weren't too many free taxis on the street, but after five or six minutes he was relieved when a cab travelling on the other side of the road did a screeching U-turn and pulled up in front of him. As he climbed into the back seat, he said, 'Grand Central Station, please.'

Chapter Thirty Eight
'The Dhow'

Thanks to the converted dhow's powerful diesel engines, the voyage up the Red Sea only took a day and a half, and it was late afternoon when the dhow dropped anchor, a mile from the Saudi coastline.

During the journey, Captain Gassim had indeed looked after the American and his beautiful wife. He'd given them his personal cabin which, although far from luxurious, did have a proper bed, as opposed to the bunks Stoneham expected. The American had enjoyed the obvious discomfort Hana Chang had shown, when it was clear they would need to share the bed. That said, neither got undressed and both slept on top.

Stoneham had spent several hours checking over the equipment Commander Aidid had provided. Two sets of white clothing, being the usual attire for pilgrims. A Glock automatic, with silencer, spare magazines and ammo. Two hand grenades, a smoke grenade and a large blade hunting knife. And most important of all, two lightweight off-road motorcycles, which Stoneham had spent most of the time checking were in perfect working order. His antics, while testing the bikes up and down the deck, gave the crew a great deal of enjoyment, especially when he incorrectly assumed Hana Chang did not know how to ride.

Clearly annoyed with his assumption, she'd said, 'Step back,' as she slipped the clutch and shot along the wooden deck, turning expertly, just before the forward handrail, then pulling a wheelie, as she roared back to the frowning American.

The bikes and all the rest of the equipment were loaded into a semi-rigid dingy, which was then lowered into the water. Two of the pirates climbed down and into the craft, both of which clearly enjoyed the sight of the Asian woman's backside, as she made her way into the boat. The glare from the American turned their attention back to steadying the dingy, as he too climbed down, then hiding their mutual sniggers as he lost his balance and fell on his arse.

The first pirate pushed the small craft away from the side of the dhow and the second fired up the powerful, Evinrude-500 outboard motor. The bow of the dingy rose as the second pirate opened up the throttle. He circled the dhow making a big show of his expertise at the controls, much to the delight and cheers of his fellow shipmates looking on. That was until a gunshot was heard. Captain Gassim held his sidearm above his head, a wisp of blue smoke emanating from the muzzle. The glaring look on his face clearly showed he was pissed-off with the antics of his men. 'Stop fucking around,' he yelled, at the top of his voice. 'Get to the beach . . . Now.'

Stoneham grinned at the result of the screamed command, and the look of fear on the faces of the two boat men. He turned to Chang and said, 'Idiots.'

Chang said nothing, and took a secure seat in the bottom of the now speeding craft.

Chapter Thirty Nine
'The Zamzam Well'

When they had been informed by MI6 of the possible terrorist attack on Mecca, the Saudis had drastically increased their security throughout the Kingdom. In Mecca, the usual police presence was seen on the streets and in the Al-Haram Mosque. There were however hundreds more officers undercover, dressed as pilgrims or locals, watching all the main areas of the desert town and places of worship.

Jack had gone over to the Al-Haram with General Kamal and Colonel Masood, to take a closer look at the area. 'The attack will be on the water supply, General. On that we can be sure,' he said.

'Yes, I'm aware that would be the terrorist's intention, my dear.'

'But we don't have an open reservoir in Mecca,' said Colonel Masood.

'So where does the water come from?' said Jack, 'I know part of the Hajj ritual is to drink from *The Zamzam Well.'*

'You have knowledge of our customs, Jack?' said the General.

'I know a little of the Hajj, sir. And what it entails for those who undertake it.'

General Kamal smiled slightly. 'Very good, my dear, very good.'

'How's the Zamzam well operated now? I doubt it's the same as it was a thousand years ago.'

The colonel also looked surprised at the Englishman's awareness, and said, 'The Zamzam is actually what you would call an Artesian well. Originally, the water was taken from below ground and fed to two cisterns, one for drinking and one for washing. Back then it was, as you would expect, a simple well surrounded by a small wall of rough stones. Now, of course, with millions of people taking the water we need to be more efficient.'

Jack nodded. 'Of course. So you must have a very large holding tank or something?'

'That's correct,' said Masood, 'Nowadays, the water is drawn with high volume pumps and stored in the main storage facility. From there it's dispersed to over a hundred drinking water outlets around the mosque.'

'Okay,' said Jack. 'Let's go and take a look at this storage facility.'

Chapter Forty
'COBRA'

FIRST DEATHS FROM KILLER VIRUS, said The Daily Mail.

UNCONTROLLABLE EPIDEMIC INEVITABLE, said The Express.

GOVERNMENT HELPLESS AGAINST VIRUS, said The Guardian.

The area around Middlesbrough had been cordoned-off. Travel in and out of the infected zone had been forbidden on pain of imprisonment, and a total curfew imposed. The presence of armed soldiers patrolling the area had fuelled massive public unrest. Rioters and looters had been arrested.

The World Health Organisation had provided specialists to help the bio-chemists from Porton Down, but the work to produce an effective antidote to the Baghdad virus would not be completed in time to save all lives.

In 10 Downing Street, the Prime Minister was chairing the fourth COBRA meeting in as many days. She looked at the men and women around the big conference table. Their stern faces said it all. No-one had any answers.

The PM looked tired. She took a deep breath and returned to the open folder on the table in front of her. 'Four hundred and sixty seven, infected. Thirty two children . . . twenty nine adults . . .' she raised her head . . . 'dead.'

The Director General of the Security Services looked at the PM. 'As you know, Prime Minister, we have deployed assets to track-down the perpetrators of this attack, and we're confident we can capture them. Once we do, an antidote will be secured, ma'am.'

The PM took another deep breath . . . 'I hope so. May God help us. I hope so.'

Chapter Forty One
'The Al-Haram Mosque'

Off the Saudi coast, the sun had almost set, as the small boat approached the shoreline. The pirate slowed the outboard motor to almost nothing, as his sidekick viewed the beach with night-vision binoculars.

'Gimme those,' said Stoneham to the man. He adjusted the setting, then scanned the shoreline from north to south. 'Looks fine. Now get us ashore.'

The pirate spun the throttle and the tiny craft surged forward. Stoneham, without his cane for balance, fell on his arse again. The two pirates looked at each other and grinned.

Once on the beach Chang kept a look-out, as the three men carefully manhandled the motor cycles out of the boat. They pushed the bikes up the soft sand and into a small clump of trees.

'Okay,' said Stoneham, 'be back here in three hours. And don't think about fucking us over. Commander Aidid is a good friend of mine.'

At the mention of Aidid's name, the grins disappeared from the pirates' faces. 'Don't worry, boss. We be back for you and the lovely lady.'

'Okay, now get the hell outta here,' said the American.

He and Chang watched as the two Somalis jogged down the beach, pushed the boat into the water and sailed away into the darkness. Stoneham checked the Glock, screwed on the silencer, and slipped it into his shoulder holster. He carefully attached one of the grenades to his belt and secured the other, along with the smoke grenade, in his rucksack.

'I'll take this,' said Chang, as she picked up the knife.

'Mind you don't cut yourself,' he said sarcastically, then attached the walking cane to his bike's handlebars.

The white pilgrim-robes were put on over their clothes and, with her head covered, they looked like any other couple on the Hajj.

They headed inland along the small beach road, towards the Jeddah-Mecca highway. With the moon now high in the sky, the wide expanse of desert was lit by silvery moonlight, and they could see the main road a mile or so in front of them. 'Great,' said Stoneham.

'What?' shouted Chang, over the noise of the engines.

'Look at the road. It's so busy. Just what we needed.'

Chang nodded and readjusted her head-covering.

They soon joined the slow-moving line of cars, trucks and buses, but managed to maintain their pace, as they rode in and out of the heavy traffic. In some places they went off-road and, on more than one occasion, Stoneham nearly knocked over several of the walking pilgrims.

Sixty five minutes after leaving the beach, they came over the hill west of the ancient city of Mecca. The sight that lay before them made Chang gasp. The huge white and gold Al-Haram Mosque gleamed like a beacon in the black Saudi night. On each side of the road, and as far as the eye could see, were lines of tents, all laid out in perfectly regimented rows, temporary accommodation for the hundreds of thousands of pilgrims during their three days of devotion.

They pulled into one of the many parking areas and left the bikes.

'Shouldn't we lock them?' said Chang. 'We don't want to have to walk back to the beach.'

Stoneham shook his head and frowned at the woman's lack of Muslim knowledge. 'Everyone here's on holy pilgrimage. No one's gonna steal anything.'

She turned away, adjusted her head-scarf again. 'Arsehole,' she said under her breath.

He put the rucksack over his shoulder, unclipped the cane from the bike and turned to Chang. 'Okay, let's go check out this mosque.'

Greg Stoneham had been to Saudi Arabia many times, but never to Mecca. He had an idea what to expect, but never realised just how massive the Hajj crowds would really be. He and Chang entered the huge open area of the beautiful Al-Haram Mosque, along with thousands of other pilgrims. The sight, as well as the sound, was overwhelming.

The mosque was essentially in two parts, the internal and the open external area, each as big as an international football stadium. The internal area was, as other mosques, used for prayer, while the outer area was where the faithful conducted the ritual circumvention of the cube-like building in the centre. The black-silk-encased central building is regarded as Allah's house on earth and it is the duty of every pilgrim to walk around the House of God seven times.

Stoneham and Chang stood in awe at the sight before them. A sea of white, made up of thousands of people, all moving as one. The noise of their feet on marble, as they shuffled reverently around the central black structure and the sound of their voices, raised in praise of their God.

Stoneham was still taking in the amazing sight, when Chang dug him in the ribs. 'When you've finished sight-seeing, d'you think we can get on with the job?'

He frowned. 'Relax. We want to blend in.'

'Blend in? We look exactly the same as everyone else.'

'Yeah, okay. Let's get on with it. Let's go find the Zamzam storage facility.'

Chapter Forty Two
'Pot-Roast'

In Washington, Henry Madsen carefully pulled into the drive of his Georgetown home and switched off the engine. The drive from the centre of the city had been longer than usual this evening, but the weather was nice and his new car was giving him a lot of pleasure. As he stepped out, he saw one of his neighbours across the street, raised his hand and shouted, 'Good evening, Mrs Connolly.'

'Evenin', Henry,' said the older lady, as she tended her roses.

'Garden is lookin' great, Mrs Connolly.'

The lady smiled and waved. 'Sure is,' then carried on snipping away at the thorny bushes.

He unlocked the front door and shouted, 'I'm home.' As he stepped into the hallway the aroma of beef hit him. 'Hmm, pot-roast,' he said with a smile.

His young son trotted down the stairs. 'Hi, Dad,' then disappeared into the lounge.

Henry dropped his briefcase by the hall-stand and walked into the kitchen. His wife Connie turned from the stove. 'Hi darling. Supper in a few minutes.'

His little daughter Lucy, rushed over and hugged him. 'Hi, honey,' he said, as he leaned down and kissed the top of her head.

'Lucy, please go tell your brother to wash-up. Supper's almost ready,' said he mother.

'And how was your day, darling?' said Henry.

She shook her head. 'Oh, don't ask. We had a bit of an issue at school, but we'll sort it out.'

'Anything I can do to help with supper? Smells great.'

'No, I'm good. Just need a pitcher of water, please.'

Henry took out a glass jug out of the cupboard, let the water run for a few seconds, then half-filled the jug. From the freezer he topped up the rest of the jug with ice-cubes, just at the kids came in.

'Okay . . . sit down, guys,' said Connie, and placed the dish of beef on the table.

'Can I have a coke, please, mom?' asked Davy.

'Sure. But only after supper. Drink water with your meal.' said his mother.

Davy picked up the jug and poured out four glasses. The ice cubes tinkled as they fell invitingly into the tumblers. As his wife served the food, Henry and his children picked up their glasses and drank the ice-cold water.

Chapter Forty Three
'Hello Again, Greg'

At the *Al-Haram Mosque,* Stoneham went to one of the many information desks and, like any other pilgrim, picked up a free guidebook. It didn't take long to discover where the Zamzam water storage facility was located. It took several minutes to walk to the building, and a couple of minutes more for Stoneham to reconnoitre. 'This way,' he said to Chang, and set off towards another building, about a hundred yards away. The sign on the long single storey structure read, MALE ABLUTIONS.

'Wait here,' said Stoneham.

Inside were several men undertaking the ritual washing. Others were using the toilet facilities. An Asian cleaning attendant mopped the spotless marble floor. Stoneham went to the farthest WC and closed the door. The cubicle was clean and the open-floor toilet, surprisingly lacked any unpleasant smells, considering the use it must have been getting. At the back of the cubicle was a wall-mounted cistern, and on the side wall, a large toilet tissue dispenser. In the corner stood a flip-top waste bin.

Stoneham took the grenade from his rucksack and eased-out the safety pin. He tilted the waste bin and carefully placed the grenade under the metal base, securing the firing clip. He took out the smoke grenade, pulled the pin and gently dropped the hissing canister into the waste bin. He left the cubicle closing the door behind him. The walking cane clack, clack, clacked on the marble floor, as he quickly left the ablution block. Outside, Chang saw him rush out and quickly joined him. 'What is it?' she said.

Stoneham spoke quickly. 'Let's get the hell outta here.'

It took several seconds for the smoke grenade to hiss-out its contents. The next pilgrim to open the door screamed when he saw the cubicle full of smoke. 'Fire!' he yelled, then knocked over several other men in his dash to the exit. The rest of the people in the toilet block rushed for the door, all except the little Asian cleaning attendant. He ran to the end of the block and looked into the cubicle. The smoke had now spread out across the floor and he could clearly see it was the waste-bin that appeared to be on fire. He leaned in and, with his mop, pulled the bin clear of the WC. As he slowly pushed the smoking bin towards the exit the hand-grenade exploded.

Stoneham and Chang were almost back at the Zamzam storage facility when they heard the explosion. Unlike everyone else around them, they did not look back.

As the emergency sirens blared, the two security officers at the entrance to the water storage facility ran towards the blazing ablution block.

Stoneham and Chang quickly walked to the main doors. He looked around. All eyes were on the burning toilet block. She tried the doors and were both surprised to find them un-locked. 'Okay,' she said, 'we're in.'

They stepped into a small foyer area and waited a few seconds. No alarms were heard, other than the emergency claxon screaming away outside.

They moved from the foyer area, through a set of double doors and into the main part of the facility. The room was as big as a football pitch, the arched roof supported by marble clad columns. The white marble walls and floor gleamed beneath hundreds of blue fluorescent strip-lights. Rows and rows of large stainless-steel tanks reflected the blue glow from the lights, as the water pumps hummed away between them.

Quickly they moved to the nearest tank. There were several valve controls and, on the top, what appeared to be a service hatch, secured with five brass manual release wing nuts. A small ladder gave access to the hatch.

'Okay, this is good,' he said, as he placed the rucksack on the floor. He looked at Chang, her face was frozen. 'What the . . .?'

'Hello again, Greg. Long time, no see,' said Jack Castle.

Stoneham turned; standing a few yards away were Castle, a Saudi officer and two other soldiers. His face said it all, surprise, shock, disbelief.

'You look a lot different to last time we met, Greg. Slimmer, no hair, and that nasty scar. The broken nose does make you look tougher though, if you were to forget about the walking cane, that is.'

'How the . . .?'

'Oh, we'll tell you how we found you later. You're gonna be spending a lot of time, talking to a lot of people now, Greg. And the lovely Colonel Chang, a pleasure to meet you, too.'

The two soldiers held automatic weapons on the terrorists, as the Saudi officer said, 'I am Major Ibrahim Masood and you are both under arrest. Please leave the bag on the floor and step away from it.'

Stoneham smiled, as if resigned to his fate, then swiftly stepped behind Chang. He drew the grenade from inside his robes and, before his captors could respond, had the pin out. The green metal cylinder rolled menacingly towards the group.

As the three Saudi's dove for cover, Jack lunged at Chang, knocking her to the floor and landing on top of her, shielding her body with his. The deadly ordinance exploded with devastating effect. A few seconds later, as the thick cordite-laden smoke cleared, Stoneham had gone. As the Angel of Death descended, one of the soldiers shouted, 'Allah . . . They've killed Colonel Masood and the English man . . .'

Chapter Forty Four
'Lucy Madsen'

It was a little after sunrise, in his Georgetown home, when Henry Madsen stepped out of the shower. He had a busy day ahead and wanted to be in the office as soon as possible. His wife Connie was still asleep, as he quietly entered the bedroom. He'd just finished dressing when he heard the awful hacking cough from his daughter's bedroom. Connie woke immediately and looked at her husband. 'Is that Lucy?'

They both ran into the little girl's room to find her on the floor, eyes wide, face bright red. Tears ran down her flushed cheeks, as she fought for breath.

'Oh, my God,' shouted Connie. She rushed to her daughter and scooped her up in her arms. 'Darling, darling, what is it?'

Lucy couldn't speak. The awful cough sucked the oxygen from her tortured lungs. She gasped for air, as her mother cradled her. 'Oh, my God, George. Get a doctor.'

The area in front of the Emergency Department was choked with cars and ambulances.

'What the hell is this?' said George, as he tried to get near the entrance.

'Leave the car here,' screamed Connie, 'Carry her.'

He drove the car up onto the grass bank, and squeezed in between two big 4x4's, smashing his headlight in the process. He couldn't get out of the driver's door and scrambled over the passenger seat. Connie, with her child in her arms was out and stumbling towards the emergency entrance.

'Gimme her,' shouted George.

The scene in the emergency room was total chaos. Doctors, nurses, admin-staff were swamped by the huge influx of patients There were more than a hundred people, all with young children in the same distressed condition as Lucy, coughing, crying, shouting.

'Oh, my God,' said Connie, as she took in the sight before her.

A young man in a set of blue scrubs rushed up to them, a small green oxygen cylinder under his arm. 'What's her name?' he said, as he held the plastic mouthpiece over her nose and mouth.

Tears of relief streamed down George's face. 'Lucy . . . Lucy Madsen. She ten years old.'

Chapter Forty Five
10 Days Later
'No, Sir'

Lisa Reynard was on her way to Fort Mead, on the outskirts of Washington. An earlier road accident had closed part of the Maryland Beltway, so the journey had taken almost two hours. As she eventually pulled up to the main entrance of the National Security Agency, she checked her watch. Almost forty-five minutes late. She parked-up in one of the reserved slots, just as the rain began to fall. She locked the car and then jogged to the central building. After clearing Security she took the express lift to the top floor.

In the outer office, she quietly chatted to her boss's secretary. 'I did tell him you were caught-up on the beltway,' said the secretary. 'Can I get you anything while you wait?'

Lisa smiled and shook her head. 'No, I'm good, thanks.'

'Okay,' said the secretary. The phone beeped. 'Sir? Yes, sir.' She turned to Lisa and nodded to the big double doors. 'You can go in now.'

'Lisa, good to see you again,' said the NSA chief. 'Have a seat, please.'

'Thank you, sir. Sorry I'm late. I . . .'

He raised his hand and stopped her. 'That's okay. Now let's get right to it. We have a special assignment for you, Lisa.' He passed an open folder across the desk. 'This is a summary of the mission. Other details will be forwarded to your secure smartphone and my secretary has your cover documents.'

'Yes, sir,' she said, and picked up the folder.

The man watched as she read through the document, his eyes narrowed as he waited for her to finish.

She closed the folder and placed it on the desk. 'No. sir.'

Her boss frowned. 'Excuse me?'

'No, sir. I cannot undertake such a mission. That's not what I do.'

He stood up, walked around the big desk and sat on the corner. He looked at her, his eyes like slits. 'You are an NSA asset, Reynard. You're part of the United States Security Services, and you'll do whatever is required of you.'

'No, sir. I will not.'

The look on the man's face changed and became less menacing. 'Not to put too fine a point on it, Lisa. You've killed people before.'

'Yes, sir. But not in cold-blood. I'm not an assassin. And, with respect, sir, I've served this agency and my country well. I have the scars from being shot in Moscow, and I'd be dead now if it weren't for the intervention of a British agent.'

'Yes, yes, I know you were badly wounded, Lisa. And I know all about Jack Castle saving your life.'

'So again, and with respect, sir, I will not accept this mission.'

Her boss stood up and went to the window. The rain was heavy now and it blurred the view as it beat against the panes. 'Strange weather for this time of year,' he said quietly.

'Sir?'

He turned back to Lisa. 'The target has attacked the United States, with the intention of killing as many of our citizens as possible. This is not a cold-blooded assassination. This is retribution for a mass-murderer.'

She looked at the man for several seconds and said nothing.

He picked up the folder and returned to his chair. 'Your plane leaves at nineteen hundred hours, this evening. If you're on it, I wish you good luck. If you're not, then we'll address that issue in due course. Now if you'll excuse me. Good afternoon, Lisa.'

United Airways flight 113, touched down in Toronto an hour and fifteen minutes after leaving Washington. Lisa had thought all afternoon about the mission she'd been given. Even on the taxi ride to the airport, her concerns gnawed away at her. *He's right*, she thought to herself, *I have killed. But this isn't me. Sure I'm tough and resourceful. Sure, I could do what was ordered. Yeah, the target had killed Americans. And what they did to Jack . . . but that didn't make it right. It's still morally wrong for god's sake.* 'Fuck,' she said out-loud.

The driver turned his head slightly and said over his shoulder, 'You say something, miss?'

'No. Sorry. Just talkin' to myself.'

It was only when she reached the Boarding Gate did she finally decide to proceed. On the flight to Toronto she'd gone over the brief which had been sent to her secure smartphone. She was to fly to Canada under her own name, then board an Aeroflot flight to Moscow using the cover documents she'd picked up from her boss's secretary. From Moscow she'd take the first available flight to Pyongyang.

Chapter Forty Six
'Louise Reno'

Lisa slept fitfully on the ten hour flight from Moscow to North Korea. Each time she drifted-off a strange, and decidedly unpleasant, dream filled her sleeping mind . . . *She was on the sidewalk in front of the White House. A warm, sunny day. She held a lace handkerchief over her mouth and nose, as she watched people in grotesque masks and strange protective suits, pile dozens of dead bodies onto the White House lawn . . .then the body of her dead friend, Jack Castle, bloodied and broken, was thrown onto the top of the huge pile of now rotting corpses.*

'Would you like to eat now, madam?'

Lisa opened her eyes and looked at the smiling face of the steward. 'No. No thank, you,' she said, 'I'd like a whisky though. A large one, please.'

'Certainly,' said the steward as he walked away.

It was late evening when Lisa's plane touched down at Sunan International. The in-flight dream had shaken her a little but, after a stiff scotch, she quickly regained her composure and, by the time she presented her documents to the Immigration Officer, she was in full covert mode.

She handed her passport to the surly, uniformed woman, behind the desk. 'Louise Reno?' said the officer, as she suspiciously flicked through the passport. 'You are Canadian?'

Lisa smiled confidently. 'Yes, ma'am. Well, French-Canadian.'

'You have travelled from Toronto?'

'Yes, ma'am. Via Moscow.'

'I know that,' said the officer, in a not too friendly voice.

'Sorry?' said Lisa.

As if talking to a child the officer continued. 'I know you travelled via Moscow. You have just disembarked the Aeroflot flight.'

'Yes. Yes, of course. Sorry.'

'The purpose of your visit to Pyongyang?'

'Business. I have a travel company. I hope to interest tourists to come to North Korea'

The woman stared at Lisa for several seconds . . . 'Tourists?' . . . then thumped the stamp onto her passport. 'Welcome to North Korea.'

It was almost ten o'clock when Lisa finally cleared Customs and left Sunan Airport. The evening was warm and pleasant, with a light breeze coming off the Taedong River. The rank was full of taxis, none of which seemed interested in having her business. She walked to the front of the line and leaned in. 'Yanggakdo Hotel?'

The old man at the wheel nodded and started the engine, as Lisa climbed in the back. The battered and rattling taxi took almost forty minutes to make the journey from the airport to the hotel. On more than one occasion she thought it was about to splutter its last.

Situated on a verdant, narrow island in the centre of the Taedong River, and standing fifty storeys high, the hotel is one of the major landmarks of Pyongyang. Built in the late eighties, it is one of the more modern establishments in the city and is heavily patronised by the more affluent of North Korean society and high ranking military. According to her brief, the target frequently used the gym at the Yanggakdo.

Lisa paid and tipped the old taxi driver, and was rewarded with a broad toothless grin. She climbed the wide marble steps and entered the huge foyer-bar area. No one approached her to help with luggage. Almost everyone was dressed in uniform of some kind, although there were several small groups of what appeared to be businessmen, all chattering away in their high-speed Asian tongue. The atmosphere was thick with cigarette smoke and the only air- conditioning seemed to come from open windows and the main door.

At the reception desk Lisa was greeted by a pleasant, round-faced young lady. 'Good evening, madam. Welcome to the Yanggakdo Hotel.'

Lisa returned the smile. 'Louise Reno. I have a room booked for a few nights.'

The girl nodded and checked the computer. 'Your passport please, madam.'

Lisa handed over the document and waited.

'We will keep this until your departure, madam. Please sign here. You're in, 510.'

Lisa signed in and picked up her room key.

'The lift is just around the corner.' added the receptionist.

In room 510 Lisa checked the bed. The linen was clean but, with only a thin mattress on top of a solid wooden frame, the bed had no spring to it at all. 'Oh, lovely,' she said.

The TV didn't work and there was no hot water in the shower. The towels were threadbare and the carpet had several stains of dubious origin. Thankfully the window was easy to open and the fresh air made a welcome addition to the Spartan facilities.

After a very quick, cold shower, she dressed and headed back down to the foyer.

'Where's the gym, please?' she asked the round faced receptionist.

'Follow the corridor to the end and then to the left, madam,' the girl looked at her watch, 'but it will close at eleven o'clock.'

'That's, okay. I just want to have a look for now.'

The gym, to Lisa's surprise, was very well equipped and devoid of any unpleasant odours, probably due to the many windows that were open. A couple of men were still working out and the appearance of the good looking Western woman threw one of them off his stride, causing him to stumble on the running machine.

She found the changing rooms and entered the female one. Lockers, benches, and a communal shower area. *Jesus*, she thought to herself, *I hope I'm not here for too long.*

She left the gym and headed back to the bar area. The clientele was thinning out, with only a few military types and the odd businessman remaining. She ordered a whisky and took it up to her room. Upstairs, she sat in front of the open window and enjoyed the cool breeze coming in from the river. She sipped her drink, then took out her smartphone and tapped in the secure PIN. The briefing files came up and she flicked through the screens. She stopped on the picture of the target and studied the woman's face, then said quietly, 'Let's hope you're here soon, Colonel Chang.'

Chapter Forty Seven
'No Lycra For This Lady'

To maintain her cover, Lisa arranged for a car and driver to show her the city and surrounding countryside. She was sure the driver would be questioned about her movements, so she played up the concept of Pyongyang as a tourist destination, with the resulting influx of hard currency.

In the evening, as soon as the gym opened at six o'clock, she was in her training gear and working out. The first night resulted in nothing more than being hit-on by several of the younger men and, by the time the place closed at eleven, she was pretty exhausted. After five hours in the gym, not even the hard bed could keep her awake.

On the third evening, the gym wasn't as busy as the previous night, and the approaches from the male patrons had ceased. Indeed this evening there seemed to be more women than men. Lisa had been on the running-machine for a little over an hour when, just after seven o'clock, her target came in.

Hana Chang was dressed in what appeared to be new white trainers, loose fitting sweat-pants and a baggy T-shirt. Her thick black hair was tied back in a secure bun.

Her ensemble was finished off with a clean, white towelling sweat band around her head.

No Lycra for this lady, thought Lisa.

Chang didn't acknowledge anyone as she entered the gym and went straight into a stretching and twisting routine. The jogging-machine next to Lisa was out of order, but the next one mysteriously became available, swiftly vacated by the young man, on seeing Chang approach.

Chang set the speed and checked her watch, then began her routine. She'd only been running for a few minutes, when she looked to the side and noticed Lisa. 'Not seen you here before. You a resident?'

Lisa smiled and feigned a winded condition. 'Yeah . . . Here for a few days.'

'You're American?'

Lisa sucked in a breath and shook her head. 'Canadian.'

'Ah,' said Chang, with a smile. 'I'm Hana.'

'Louise,' said Lisa, 'Louise Reno.'

For the next hour the women ran alongside one another, their training interspersed with small talk and several admiring glances from Chang. At eight o'clock she looked at her watch, and then switched off the machine. 'That's enough for me.'

'Me too,' said Lisa, as her machine slowed down.

Chang picked up her bottle of energy drink and cracked the seal, then offered it to Lisa.   'Need some of this?'

'Oh, yes please. Would you mind?'

'Please, go ahead,' said Chang, as she handed over the bottle.

Lisa took a big swallow. 'Mmmmm. That's good.' She wiped the top of the bottle and passed the drink back.

Chang put the bottle to her lips and finished the contents, her eyes on Lisa the whole time.

'Mmmm, your right. That's good. Okay. Shower time,' said the Korean.

There were no other women in the changing room. Lisa and Chang stripped off their sweat- soaked clothes, took towels from their respective sports-bags and entered the communal shower.

'The water here's not too bad this time of evening,' said Chang, as she pulled the band from her head. As her hair fell down her back, she stepped under the tepid shower. Lisa turned on her water and smiled. 'Yeah, it's not too bad at all.' She opened her shampoo and began to wash her hair.

'Could I have a little of that too, Louise?'

Lisa moved closer and handed over the container. 'Sure, honey.'

Chang took the bottle and their fingers touched for a second. She looked into Lisa eyes and said, 'You're in great shape. You have a lovely figure, but what's this? Looks like a bullet wound,' she gently touched the scar on Lisa's abdomen.

Lisa didn't pull away. 'It is.'

'Sounds like the tourist business can be pretty dangerous, Louise?'

'Nothing to do with work. I was mugged.'

'Ah,' said Chang as she gently ran her finger around the scar. 'Then you are very lucky to be alive.'

'Don't I know it,' said Lisa, as she slipped back under her shower.

They chatted and laughed as they dressed, and then dried each other's hair. As they walked towards the main foyer area, Chang said, 'You have any plans for supper, Louise?'

Lisa laughed. 'Was gonna see if there was anything edible here. I've pretty much been livin' on fruit and energy bars since I arrived.'

'Well, it's the weekend and I'm free until Monday. Would you like to eat with me at my place?'

'That would be lovely. Thank you, Hana.'

Chang smiled. 'Okay, that's great. We can eat, and then you can tell me all about the tourist business.'

'Do you mind if I dash upstairs and change?'

'Of course not. I'll bring my car to the front door and meet you outside.'

'Right,' said Lisa, with a beaming smile. 'See you in a few minutes.'

Chapter Forty Eight
Another Ten Days Later
'Thunder & Lightning'

The storm over Berkshire was getting worse. On the A33 the windscreen wipers swished back and forth at top speed, but the rain was so heavy it was almost impossible to see. There was no other vehicle on the road at this time of night. The big Jaguar was doing almost eighty as it screeched off the main road and onto the lane to East Monkton. The roar of the powerful engine was dwarfed by a clap of thunder, and a flash of lightning turned the night sky to day.

The car was two hundred yards from the entrance as it took the last bend in the lane. The pool that always formed there in heavy rain caught the front wheels and the speeding vehicle began to aquaplane. The laws of physics took over. Jack fought with the steering, but the Jaguar was now master of his destiny as it bounced over the grass verge and into the four hundred year old oak. As the big car smashed into the huge old tree, it seemed as though the thunder and lightning applauded the inevitable accident.

The airbags deployed with a bang and hit him hard in the face. The car bounced off the tree, spinning wildly as it splashed into the small stream running alongside the lane. His head hit the side of the car as it came to rest and he felt the warm trickle of blood run down the side of his face. The seat belt was jammed, so he reached for the penknife he kept in the armrest. The car was filling with water, as the storm-swollen stream flooded in through the smashed screen. He cut through the webbed belt and pulled himself out through the opening, as another flash of lighting lit up the crash scene. His breathing was heavy and his heart pounded as he scrambled up the slippery banking. Back on the road he began to run, the lightning appeared to drive him on.

The wound to his head throbbed and the blood gushed down his rain-beaten face. At last he was at the big gates. He took hold of the bars and rattled the solid steel; nothing moved. He rushed to the intercom and banged on the button, but heard nothing except the ear-shattering noise of the thunder overhead.

A flash of lightning lit up something on the drive, but in a second the darkness returned and engulfed the big house. He pulled himself up onto the first rung of the ornate gates, but the rain and his breathless condition were no match for the wet metal. He slipped and caught his inner bicep on one of the spikes, cutting deep into the muscle. Again he made to climb the slick steel as the lightning crackled and flashed above.

At last he was at the top, but lost his balance; he hung on with the strength he had left but, as he threw the other leg over, slipped. The top spike went into his thigh, viciously impaling him. The pain was unbelievable as his flesh tore and he fell to the hard gravel.

Disoriented, winded and bleeding, he manged to stand. The pain in his head and leg forgotten as he ran, heart pounding, towards the house. A few yards from the door he tripped over something and fell face-down on the driveway. As he rolled over, the lightning again lit up the storm-wracked night, revealing the body of Brian, his security man, a large black hole in the centre of his forehead.

Jack wiped the blood from his eyes and limped through the open door into the large hallway. The lightning lit up the hall and brought him to a complete stop. Slumped against the wall was the body of his brother Mathew, his white shirt soaked in blood from the dozen bullet holes in is chest. Jack turned and entered the elegant drawing room. The blazing log fire illuminated the dreadful scene before him. His friends, Tom Hillman and Lisa Reynard were slumped in the fireside armchairs, eyes wide open, their throats cut from ear to ear.

His heart was almost beating out of his chest, he almost vomited. He turned and staggered to the wide staircase, struggled to climb the thick carpeted steps. At the top he made to turn to his bedroom and then saw the nursery door wide open. On legs of lead, he slowly entered the pretty room.

As if to welcome him to the horrendous scene, the thunder roared it's loudest and a brilliant flash of lightning lit up the nursery.

His family lay slaughtered. His wife Nicole and his beautiful twins lay dead in front of him. Nicole, with her arms around the children, cradled her daughters in death.

He fell to his knees, a scream building from deep in his soul. He tried to scream, but the muscles contracted in his throat, he was choking, and then it came, a noise so awful, like a dying animal, caught in a deadly trap . . . 'Ahhhhhhhh'

'Doctor! Doctor! He's awake.'

Chapter Forty Nine
'Three Weeks In A Coma'

Jack tried to speak, but the tube in his throat made it impossible. He opened his eyes and saw the beautiful face of Nicole.

'Zaikin,' she said, as she leaned down and gently kissed his lips. A glistening tear trickled down her cheek and fell onto his.

A doctor and nurse entered the room. 'Excuse me, Nicole,' said the doctor.

Nicole moved away from the bed.

'Hello, Jack. I'm Doctor Mitchell. You've been in a coma for three weeks. We're going to check you over now and then we'll get rid of that tube. Make you a little more comfortable. Just relax for a moment or two.'

The nurse turned to Nicole and smiled. 'Would you like to wait outside, please?'

She moved to the side of the room and shook her head. 'I'm staying.'

The nurse smiled and nodded. 'Okay.'

Mitchell leaned over Jack and flicked a small flashlight on and on off into each of Jack's eyes. 'Excellent response.'

The nurse made a note on an iPad. She took his wrist and checked the pulse, her eyes focused on the little watch clipped to her uniform. Again she made a note on the iPad.

Another nurse entered with a trolley laid out with several items of medical equipment.

'Okay, Jack. Let's get this out of you,' said the doctor.

Nicole couldn't see what was happening, but she could hear Jack's moans, as the tube was drawn from his throat. Another tear ran down her cheek.

After the procedure, the nurses left the room. The doctor took a seat next to the bed.

'Waaawaa,' Jack tried to speak.

'Just relax,' said the doctor.

A look of panic flashed across Jack's face, as he tried to speak again. 'Waaalarrr.'

The doctor put his hand on Jack's forearm.

Nicole came over to the bed and held Jack's other hand.

'Zaikin, it's alright. Let the doctor explain.'

'You've sustained several injuries Jack,' said Mitchell. 'But I can assure you, none are life-threatening. Well, not now anyway.'

'Baaarrrwww.'

'Don't try to speak, Zaikin. Listen to the doctor.'

Mitchell smiled. 'Thank you, Nicole,' He looked at Jack and continued. 'D'you remember what happened in Saudi?'

Jack nodded slightly.

'Excellent. The grenade did quite a bit of damage but, as I said, not now life-threatening. There was a large piece of shrapnel removed from your left thigh. Muscle and tissue damage only, no bones broken. Another piece removed from your inner bicep and again no bone damage. Several smaller fragments removed from your left torso and shoulder. Everything is healing well, but you're going to have a couple of nasty scars on your leg and arm.

Nicole smiled and gently squeezed Jack's hand. 'I'm sure they'll look very sexy.'

'Now,' said Mitchell. 'They removed a piece of shrapnel from your skull, about the size of an olive. Fortunately, it did not do any damage to the brain. The cavity however was an issue. In the past it would have been closed up with a plate, but the Saudi surgeons used a new procedure, that will result in a full and complete regeneration of the skull damage.'

Jack's eyes narrowed. 'Daaamaaggg.'

'Just listen, darling.' said Nicole.

The doctor raised Jack's left arm slightly. The hand was heavily bandaged. 'They amputated the distal phalange, the last part of your little finger, and used the bone to close up the cavity in the skull. All very cutting edge, if you'll pardon the pun.'

Jack moved his right hand to his mouth and tapped his lips.

'Your speech will return in a few days, Jack. There's still a little swelling around the base of the skull, but as I said, it'll subside completely in the next few days.'

More tears ran down Nicole's cheeks, as she felt Jack squeeze her hand and smile.

The medication to relieve the swelling in the skull had completely wiped him out. It was late afternoon the following day, when Jack woke from a thirty hour sleep. He opened his eyes and saw Nicole asleep in the chair. 'Heyyy,' he said drowsily.

She jumped at the sound of his voice, and rushed to the bed. 'Zaikin,' she gently kissed his lips. 'How're you feeling, my darling?'

'Betttaa.' he struggled to get the word out. 'Wattaa . . . pleees.'

'Yes,' she said, as she held the drinking cup to his lips.

'Werrrs, twwiinnz?'

'I'll bring the girls when your speech has returned, darling. They send their love to their daddy.'

Jack's eyes watered, as he said, 'I missss thmmm.'

She touched his cheek. 'I know you do, Zaikin.'

A nurse entered. 'Ah, Mr Castle. Good to see you awake.' She took his pulse. 'And how are we today?'

'Want go howwmm.'

The nurse, smiled. 'You'll be home soon. You're doing very well.'

'Glaaad yu thinn so.'

The nurse gave a little laugh. 'No sense-of-humour loss, then.'

'How is he?' said Nicole.

'Pulse is good and strong. I'll change his dressings once your visitors go.'

'Visitors?' said Nicole.

'Yes. They've been here a couple of hours. Should I ask them to come in?'

Nicole nodded. 'Thank you, nurse.'

A couple of minutes later Mathew entered, followed by Lisa Reynard and the nurse.

Mathew hugged Nicole and kissed her cheek, then turned to his brother. 'Still in bed then?'

Lisa hugged Nicole and then held her hand; both had tears in their eyes. 'He's tough, honey,' said Lisa, then turned to Jack. 'Hello, handsome.'

'Would you like to sit up?' asked the nurse.

'Mmmm,' said Jack.

The nurse, assisted by Nicole, gently raised him and adjusted the pillows at his back.

'I'll be back later to change your dressings.' She smoothed down his bedding then turned to the visitors. 'Don't tire him, please,' she said protectively, then left the room.

'Some minder you've got there,' said Mathew, with a grin.

'Waattar plees.'

Nicole helped him as he drank from the cup.

'Lizaaa waaa yu dooin heer?'

She smiled and put her hand on his shoulder. 'What do you think? Came to see you.'

Jack smiled, then winked. 'Thaank yu . . .' He turned to his brother, his face a testament to the pain in his head. 'Vayrush?'

'The virus?' said Mathew.

Jack nodded slightly, his eyes narrowed with the pain of moving.

'Everything's okay, Jack. Let's talk about it in a few days, when you feel better.'

'Tel mi naaow.'

Mathew looked at Nicole. 'Tell him,' she said, 'he'll only worry otherwise.'

Mathew sat down next to the bed. 'You've been out of it for over three weeks, Jack. You remember what happened in the Zamzam storage facility?'

Jack slowly nodded.

'Stoneham's grenade killed Major Masood and one of his men.'

'Ohhh no . . .'

'But when you dived on Chang, you took most of the blast and you saved her life.'

'Stowwnnumm?'

'Stoneham got away, but Ryan Lafferty has gone after him.'

Jack closed his eyes, then bowed his head. A few seconds later he looked at Mathew and said, 'The vayrush?'

Mathew smiled, 'Is under control now. We secured the antidote.'

'Chaangzz blooddd?'

'No. We couldn't use Chang's blood to produce a serum. She had a hepatitis strain. Her blood was useless.'

'So haaww?'

Mathew looked at Lisa, then back to his brother. 'We traded her for the antidote, Jack. We did a deal with General Chang. He gave us the formula.'

Jack closed his eyes just as the protective nurse came back. 'That's enough, now. Look at him. He's exhausted.'

Mathew stood up, as the nurse all but pushed him out of the way. 'Oaky, Jack, we'll talk later,' he said.

Chapter Fifty
'Welcome Home'

After being in a coma for three weeks and a further week in the hospital, Jack was more than happy to eventually return to East Monkton. Mathew had arranged an escorted car for Jack, but Nicole insisted on taking her husband home herself.

It was mid-afternoon when Nicole's Range Rover pulled up to the front of the big house. The sky was cloudless and the sun warm as Jack stepped out of the car. He was overwhelmed with emotion when he saw the reception committee waiting for him. Relief to be home, joy at the sight of his family, regret he'd put himself in such a dangerous position, but most of all joy, in the welcome his two beautiful daughters gave as they rushed to him. Nicole saw the tears in his eyes, as he scooped up the giggling girls.

'Welcome home, boss,' said Brian.

'Good to have you home, Mr Jack,' said Brian's wife, Maggie

Svetlana came over and, uncharacteristically, hugged him. 'I'm please you are safe, Mr Jack.'

Last to greet him was Lisa Reynard. With an overtly Southern American drawl, she said, 'Welcome home, Mr

Jack, sir.' Then, with a wink and a smile, she kissed his cheek. 'Good to see you, honey.'

'Wow,' said Jack, 'I'll have to get banged-up a bit more if I'm gonna get such welcomes.'

Nicole frowned. 'I don't think so, mister.'

'Can I get you anything, Mr Jack?' said Maggie.

'I could murder a nice cuppa tea, please, Maggie.'

With a big smile, she said, 'Already laid out in the drawing room.'

The rest of the day was spent with Nicole, the twins, and Lisa. Most of the time, at the insistence of the girls, Jack was on the carpet playing with various dolls, ponies and games. By the time Svetlana returned at seven, to take the girls up to the nursery, he was worn out.

After good-night kisses were given to mummy, daddy and Aunty Lisa, the little ones dashed off with the nanny.

'We're not out for dinner, are we?' said Jack.

'I haven't booked anything. But we could go down to the pub, if you like?' said Nicole.

'No. Prefer to stay home tonight. Right, I'm gonna get a shower before dinner,' he said.

'Okay, darling.'

After he left, Lisa said. 'He looks good. Lost some weight though.'

Nicole smiled. 'Yes, he has. I'm glad he's home at last.' Her smartphone beeped. She swiped the screen. 'Hi Dad . . . Yes, we're all fine, darling . . . Yes, he's home .

. . Okay . . . Okay . . . No it's fine . . . I will . . . I will . . .
Talk soon. Love you.'

'Dimitri?' said Lisa.

'Yeah. Just checking Jack's home. He sends his
regards to you as well.'

'Where is he?'

'He's at his steel mill in Japan, again.'

'Oh, nice,' said Lisa. 'Okay, think I'll have a bath.
Dinner at eight?'

'Yes, eight.'

Lisa hugged Nicole, winked, and said, 'Go on up, and
wash your boy's back. See you later.'

Chapter Fifty One
'Be Careful'

Jack had been home for five days when he got the call from Mathew. The time on the smartphone read 06:10. He swiped the screen. 'Mornin, Matt.'

'Morning, Jack. How are you feeling, bro?'

'A lot better. The odd headache, but a couple o' Paracetamol usually fixes it.'

'Feel ready to get back into the fray then?'

'Sure. What's the latest?'

'Ryan Lafferty's been in contact. They believe they've got a positive lead on Mr Stoneham.'

'That's great, Matt. You want me to come in to the office?'

'No need. I'll ask Victoria to get you and Lisa a flight to Istanbul today.'

'What about the Yanks? Have you told them we have a lead?'

'Not yet. I'll wait 'til you and Lisa are on station. Don't want them sending in the heavy mob. Stoneham would suss that and just disappear again.'

'Okay, good. I'll be in contact after we talk to Ryan. Anything else, Matt?'

'That's it for now. Just be careful, big brother.' Mathew heard Jack chuckle.

The line went silent.

The sun was already up and beginning to show over the tall conifers on the east side of the garden. Jack opened the patio doors and went out. He could feel the warm rays on his face. He sucked in a deep breath and looked around the beautifully kept gardens, surrounding the big house. 'This is the last time,' he said quietly.

'Last time for what?' said Nicole.

Jack turned, he hadn't heard her come up behind him. She put her head against his chest, her arms round his neck. 'Last time?'

'Tell you later, Nikki. It's early, darling. Go back to bed. The girls won't be up for a while yet.'

'No, they won't.' She kissed him and linked her arm through his. 'Come on then.'

'You go on up, babe. I'm not tired.'

She squeezed up against him. 'Nor am I, big man. Come on.'

The chauffeured car arrived just after eleven o'clock. At the front of the house Nicole and Lisa kissed cheeks. 'It's been great to spend this time with you, Nikki. Thank you,' said Lisa. 'See you again soon.'

'You too, darling,' said Nicole. 'You're always welcome, anytime. The girls love having Aunty Lisa here. And so do we,' they hugged again and Nicole whispered, 'Look after him.'

'Sure, honey. Sure,' whispered Lisa, then climbed into the big Jaguar.

Jack put his arms around her and said. 'Don't worry, Nikki. I'll be home soon. I love you, my darling.'

'I love you too, Zaikin. Be careful.'

Chapter Fifty Two
'Rasputin'

The Turkish Airways flight to Istanbul was delayed by over an hour. Jack and Lisa waited in the packed Business Class Lounge and chatted about anything, other than the mission. Eventually the flight departed a little before three-thirty.

After lunch, as the other passengers settled down to read, sleep, or watch movies, Jack and Lisa spoke quietly. Mathew had kept them up-to-date with Ryan Lafferty's progress in the search for, and eventual discovery of, Mr Gregory Stoneham's location.

Lafferty, using the pseudonym, Rasputin, had trawled the Dark-Web, and made it known he was recruiting specialist mercenaries for an extremely lucrative, yet high risk mission in Bulgaria. He'd been contacted by dozens individuals, none of which sounded, or felt like, Stoneham. After almost three weeks in the tiny Moscow apartment, his efforts bore fruit and he was sure he'd made contact with the rogue agent's intermediary.

Ryan had then travelled from Moscow to Istanbul and was now awaiting the arrival of Jack and Lisa, in the Irish Bar of Ataturk Airport.

The laborious Immigration and Customs formalities over, Jack and Lisa eventually came out into the very busy Arrivals Hall. It took a few seconds for Jack to spot Ryan standing quietly by the exit doors. 'There he is.'

Like any other couple, Lisa linked her arm through Jack's, and the two eased their way through the crowds of eager people waiting for their friends and loved ones.

As Lafferty saw them approach, he turned and slowly left the terminal. Once outside he picked up the pace and headed for the main car-park, quickly followed by Jack and Lisa.

In the ground floor of the multi-storey, Jack saw the lights of an old Mercedes flash. As they approached the old vehicle Lisa looked around, a few people with bags and luggage, loading and unloading cars, nothing out of place or untoward. The rear door was open and they both quickly scrambled in.

'Good to see you again, Ryan,' said Jack. 'This is Lisa Reynard. Lisa, meet Ryan Lafferty.'

'Nice t'see ya again, Jack. For sure, it's a pleasure to meet ya too, Lisa.'

She smiled, his lilting Irish brogue and boyish charm, clearly not lost on her. 'Shame it's not under more enjoyable circumstances,' she said.

'You're right there, Lisa. Okay, let's get the hell outta here.'

The drive from the airport to the city was good, and although the roads were extremely busy, Istanbul's new infrastructure kept the traffic moving swiftly, until they got into the old city area. Lafferty had rented a small but well-located apartment in the upmarket district of Beyoğlu, on the European side of the Bosphorus. Being one of the older parts of Istanbul and bordering on the water's edge, Beyoğlu is now a thriving area for tourists, and up-market shops, cafes and restaurants. The perfect place for them to blend in amongst the thousands of other Westerners and tourists.

The apartment was on the top floor of a three storey building and the view, from the small lounge, looked out across the Bosphorus, to the Asian side.

'Wow,' said Lisa, as she took in the vista. 'What a view.'

'Sure is,' said Lafferty. 'Not a bad little gaff, but we only have two bedrooms. The couch here, turns into a bed though.'

'It's fine, Ryan,' said Jack.

'Can I get you guys anythin'?' said Ryan.

'Some water, please,' said Lisa.

'Cuppa tea would be great,' said Jack.

'Comin up,' said the smiling Irishman, and disappeared into the small kitchen.

Lisa turned from the window. 'He's a real charmer.'

Jack grinned, 'He sure is, to be sure, to be sure.'

Lisa raised her eyebrows and shook her head.

With water and tea served, the three sat down.

'So. Where are we, Ryan? What's the deal?' said Jack.

Lafferty leaned forward and took a sip of steaming black tea. 'I've made contact with the intermediary Stoneham uses. It's the same one I was in contact with in the past.'

'How d'you know that?' said Lisa, 'if you've only communicated on-line?'

'The way he chats. The way he uses certain phrases. He has a habit o' referrin' to people as, *My Friend*.'

'So when do you meet him?' said Jack.

'Tomorrow night. But there's a wee problem there.'

'Oh yeah?' said Lisa.

'Ye'see, I've met this joker before. So I can't pitch up again. He'll be off-on-his-toes, the minute he lays eyes on me.'

'Right,' said Jack, 'so it's fair to say he doesn't know whether to expect a man or a woman? if every thing's been done on-line?'

'Aye, that's true. He only knows me as, Rasputin.'

Lisa smiled slightly. 'Very colourful.'

Jack finished his tea. 'I could meet him, but there's a chance Stoneham may be close-by. If he is and he sees me, then, as you so eloquently put it, Ryan, he'll be off-on-his-toes, as well.'

'Okay,' said Lisa,' I guess tomorrow night, Rasputin, will be a woman.'

Chapter Fifty Three
'The Sultan Club'

It was a few minutes to eleven when Lisa arrived at *The Sultan Club*. Dressed in a short jacket, black jeans, blouse and high heels, she looked casual, borderline-classy. The well-built doorman watched as she got out of the taxi.

'Hi, there,' she said, as he held the big door open.

In the foyer, an attractive young woman sat behind a small desk, her low cut gown leaving nothing to the imagination. She smiled, and said, 'Member, or guest?'

Lisa returned the smile. 'Guest, I suppose,'

'That will be thirty euros, please.'

Lisa paid, said, 'Thank you,' then walked across to the next door. Another heavy-set man held it open. 'Have a great evening, miss,' said the big man.

Lisa smiled. 'Thank you.' Once inside the club, she said quietly, 'Anybody there?'

Through the tiny earpiece she heard Jack's voice. 'Reading you loud n' clear, babe. Any problems and we'll be in there in twenty seconds.'

She'd been told the club would not be too busy at this time of night. She went to the bar and, again as she'd been told, ordered a Rasputin Cocktail. The girl behind the bar looked at her and said, 'Sorry I don't know that one?'

Lisa leaned forward and in a loudish voice, said, 'Straight vodka in a glass, with another one next to it.'

The girl grinned. 'Cool. I like it.' She put two glasses on the counter and poured the drinks. 'That's twenty euros, please.'

Lisa was about to pay when a man leaned in and dropped a twenty euro note next to the drinks. 'I love Rasputin Cocktails,' he said.

Lisa turned to face him. 'It's all I drink.'

The man picked up the glasses and smiled. 'We have a booth over here.'

They sat down in one of the darker areas of the club, well away from the dance floor.

He handed her a glass and chinked his against it. 'Cheers.' He knocked the vodka back in one, then said, 'you're not what I expected, Rasputin.'

Lisa raised her glass. 'Cheers. Is that good or bad?'

The man smiled. 'Oh, for me, it's very good.'

Lisa smiled too, but not at the man next to her. She was smiling at Jack's voice in her ear. 'What a fucking sleaze-ball.'

'How about another drink before we discuss our business?' said the man.

'Sure, but make mine a beer this time.'

He waved over a waitress. 'Beer and a vodka, please,' then turned back to Lisa. 'This might turn out to be pleasure as well as business.' He put his hand on her thigh.

Lisa smiled again, as she slipped her hand into her bag. There was a metallic click and then the man felt the sharp tip of the switch-blade in his crotch. 'Don't think because I'm a woman, I'm just the help. I'm doing the hiring here. If you wanna fuck-around, I'm sure there's plenty of ladies in here who'll oblige. Now, are we gonna talk business, or d'you want whatever miniscule thing is in here,' she pressed the tip of the knife harder into his crotch, 'chopping off?'

The man raised his hands slightly. 'I'm sorry. I'm sorry.'

The waitress returned and took-in the scene before her. Lisa smiled up at the girl. 'Pay her and give her a good tip,' the knife still in the man's crotch.

He did as instructed. The waitress beamed a huge smile, and said, 'Thank you, ma'am.'

The girl left. There was a second click as the blade retracted back into the handle. Lisa picked up the bottle of beer, twisted off the cap, tapped the bottle against his glass, and said, 'Cheers.' She could hear Jack chuckling through the earpiece.

The next fifteen minutes were spent roughly outlining the fictitious mission in Bulgaria and the considerable rewards, for what essentially was a three day kidnapping job. At eleven-thirty the music changed from jazz, to a

218

classic Turkish instrumental. A spotlight came on, as a raven haired belly-dancer shimmied onto the dance floor. The audience clapped in rhythm to the music, as the girl sensually gyrated around the dance floor. She finished her show and wiggled off to the sound of applause and raucous cheers.

'You want another drink?' said the man.

Lisa shook her head. 'No, thanks. I think we're done here. Any questions?'

He shook his head. 'No, we're good. My principle will meet you at one o'clock tomorrow. The Blue Mosque, under the dome.'

Lisa stood up. 'I need to pay a quick visit.' She found the sign for LADIES and went in. She stood at the sink and turned on the water. 'You get all that, hun?'

Jack's voice came back. 'Yeah, all good. Now get the hell outta there.'

'On my way.'

The cubicle door opened and the belly-dancer came out, wearing a white towelling robe. She went to the sink and washed her hands. 'That's the first sign of madness, pet.'

'Sorry?' said Lisa.

'Talkin t' yerself.'

Lisa looked at the pretty woman and grinned. 'You're not Turkish.'

'Turkish? Nah, pet. Ah'm from Newcastle.'

Chapter Fifty Four
'Breakfast'

The following morning was overcast but warm. Jack, Lisa and Ryan had talked about today's meeting until the early hours and were confident they could capture Stoneham, if indeed it was he who showed up. Lisa came out of her room and found Ryan in the tiny kitchen. There was fresh coffee and a pot of tea on the table. He'd been out and brought back croissants, strawberries and a good size chunk of honeycomb, dripping with the golden nectar.

'Wow, this looks delicious,' said Lisa.

'Coffee?' he said.

'Oh, yes, please.'

As he filled a mug for her, she helped herself to breakfast. 'Mmm, I'm hungry. Thank's, Ryan.'

The Irishman flashed his perfect smile. 'You're very welcome.'

She went into the lounge and found Jack on the phone, sat down at the table and tucked into the food while he finished his call. 'How's Nicole?'

Jack smiled. 'Yeah, she's fine. Sends her regards, says we have to be careful.'

'Okay. You spoke to Mathew, yet?'

'Yes, I called him earlier. Briefed him on today's meeting. He said the same.'

'The same?'

'Same as Nicole. Be careful.'

Lafferty stuck his head round the kitchen door. 'Are ya wantin any breakfast, Jack?'

'Just tea, thanks, buddy.'

The three spent the morning going over the meeting and the possible variables. They all knew Stoneham would be extremely careful and the chances of him not showing were fifty-fifty. At exactly twelve noon, the *Midday Call to Prayers* was heard from the local mosque, the lilting tones of the Muezzin's voice echoed across the neighbourhood.

Jack looked at his Rolex. 'Twelve o'clock. Right, let's do one last check on the gear.'

Lisa unfastened her blouse and checked the microphone was secure between her breasts, and her ear piece firmly in position. Jack and Ryan checked their weapons. They all turned away from each other and spoke quietly. Each giving a thumbs-up their comms were good. Earpieces were removed for the time being, then Ryan said, 'Okay, folks, we'd better get a move on.'

'Let's go,' said Lisa.

'Rock n' roll,' said Jack.

Chapter Fifty Five
'Top Of The Hill'

Stoneham had listened and considered everything his intermediary had said about the woman. His instinct was to give the meeting a miss but, according to his man, the job was a simple kidnap and ransom, with a pay-check of one and a half to two million dollars for each man involved.

He'd been paid six million by the Koreans, far short of the expected twenty, due to the failed mission in Saudi. He still had over a million left from the up-front expenses. The chance of another couple of million was worth the risk of a meeting at least. Before he left he made one last phone call, then checked his gun and silencer. He looked at himself in the mirror. The wig was cheap, but it did its job, and the beard he'd grown over the last few weeks was now thick and luxurious. He slipped on his sunglasses, then picked up the black walking cane. For several seconds he admired the ornate wolf's head handle, then kissed it.

The drive to The Blue Mosque, on the other side of the Bosphorus, would take some time, so he left the villa a little before eleven. The traffic was busy as expected but, by taking the Avrasya Tunnel, he'd crossed over in less than an hour. As he drove out of the tunnel he saw the beautiful old building at the top of the hill. The road up to the mosque was choked with tourist-laden taxis, so he left the car in a disabled bay and set off walking. It was still very overcast, but the temperature was well into the high-twenties and, by the time he arrived at the main entrance, his shirt was stuck to his back and the thin cotton jacket bore sweat marks under the arms. He went to one of the many street vendors and bought two bottles of water, quickly downing one. He found a seat under one of the olive trees and checked the time, twelve-forty. His leg was bothering him after the arduous walk up the hill and, as he sat and massage his thigh, he considered the location. Dozens and dozens of tourists milling around and probably as many inside the mosque, too busy a place for a trap, too risky for a shoot-out. He opened the second bottle and sipped from it. *Two million dollars,* he said to himself. *Fuck it.*

At ten minutes to one, he entered the wonderful old mosque.

Chapter Fifty Six
'Shoot-Out'

The Sultan Ahmed Mosque, more commonly known as The Blue Mosque, was built over four-hundred years ago and remains to this day as it was then. The fabulous blue and gold tiling, its size and architecture, and the sheer awe the building inspires, is the reason it has several thousand visitors a day.

Stoneham paid the exorbitant extra entrance fee, so as not to have to wait in the queue. Once inside, he found a vantage point and spent the next five minutes scanning the fabulous interior of the building, looking for anything untoward, out of the ordinary, traps, set-ups, or anything that didn't look right.

The midday prayers had finished and the faithful were all but gone, leaving dozens of tourists to mill around and take-in the wonderful building. Couples, small groups, larger conducted parties, walked reverently around the amazing mosque.

In the very centre of the cavernous structure, and directly under the huge dome, a woman stood alone. Tall and slim, she wore an ankle length skirt, with a long-sleeved blouse. Her hair was covered with a plain white headscarf.

Stoneham slipped his hand under his jacket and felt the reassurance of the automatic beneath his armpit. He took a deep breath and slowly walked to the centre of the mosque.

The woman was facing away from him as he approached. The tap, tap, tap, of the cane on marble made her turn. She looked at him and for a few seconds nothing was said. He sensed a slight smile, and then said, 'Rasputin?'

'Yes,' said Lisa.

'That's him.' she heard Jack say. 'Forget the wig and beard. The crooked nose, the cane. It's him.'

'Good. We have some business to discuss, but I don't think I can keep calling you Rasputin,' said Stoneham.

Lisa smiled. 'Call me, Louise.'

'Can we go somewhere a little more intimate, Louise? I'm not one for standing around in public.'

Her smile got bigger and she winked. 'Sure honey.'

Stoneham frowned at her flippancy. 'What the . . . '

'We meet again, Greg,' said Jack.

Stoneham turned slowly to see Jack Castle and Shaun Maguire standing in front of him.

'Jack Castle. I thought you were dead? And, Shaun, which I'm now sure is not your real name.'

Ryan said nothing. The grin on his handsome face, said it all.

Jack had a newspaper over his hand. 'What do you think about today's news?' said Jack, as he raised the folded paper slightly.

Stoneham looked down and saw the muzzle of the gun beneath the paper. 'Nothing good in there, I guess.'

The crack of the gun-shot echoed throughout the cavernous building. Panic consumed the shuffling and silent tourists, turning them into a screaming mob, rushing for the exit.

Blood splattered onto Jack's face, as the side of Ryan's head blew open.

'Jesus!' said Lisa, and instinctively dropped to the floor.

From the corner of his blood covered eye, Jack saw the figure running towards them, gun raised and ready to fire again. Jack spun, got off two rounds, both of which missed, destroying a wall mounted statue.

The running man fired again, but this time, he missed. He was only yards away now, closing the range, ready to shoot again. Two more shots boomed out in the now panic filled mosque, but not from Jack's or the man's gun. As if in slow motion the man fell forward, his eyes wide, his arms wider, as the two heavy calibre bullets thumped into his back, tearing through his lung and lodging in his heart. He was dead before his lifeless body hit the gleaming marble floor.

Stoneham saw his chance. He set off as fast as he was able, the cane clack, clack, clacking, as he headed for the rear exit.

Jack knelt down and checked Ryan's carotid. Nothing. He turned to Lisa, 'You hit?' he shouted.

'I'm fine,' she said, as she quickly got to her feet.

Jack turned to see the source of the other gunshots. His jaw dropped slightly and his mouth fell open. General Kamal bin Usef walked up to them, a large smoking pistol in hand.

'General?' said Jack.

'Are you two okay?' he said.

'We're fine, sir. Thanks to you. But we gotta get after Stoneham.' Jack made a move to head to the exit.

'Hold on, Jack.'

'What the . . .?'

'Hold on, my dear. There's nothing to worry about. I have a couple of men back there.'

Kamal had just finished talking, when a sad looking Greg Stoneham was escorted back between two tough looking Saudis.

The sound of police sirens replaced the shouts and screams of the tourists. 'We'd better lay our weapons on the ground, my dear,' said Kamal. The two men held onto Stoneham as they carefully placed their guns on the ground. Jack and Kamal did the same then, with hands on heads, they waited for the arrival of the Turkish police.

Over two dozen heavily armed police officers rushed, yelling and shouting, into the mosque. Jack and Lisa, General Kamal and his men, along with Stoneham, were roughly handcuffed and manhandled towards the exit of the now empty building. A small team of medics appeared and unceremoniously busied themselves with the grim task of collecting Ryan Lafferty's and the shooter's bodies.

Outside, several police cars, lights flashing and sirens still blaring, waited to transfer the gun-toting foreigners to the local jail. No one spoke to the police except Stoneham, who insisted he was unable to walk while handcuffed and without his stick, a fact that was made obvious, by him ostentatiously falling over. A senior officer yelled to one of his subordinates to unshackle the stumbling man's hands and clip one cuff to his own. The stick was returned and a sombre faced Stoneham clack, clacked, from the mosque to the waiting cars.

Chapter Fifty Seven
'Where's Stoneham'

Jack was roughly pushed into the back of the police car. An officer climbed in beside him and another got into the driver's seat. Lisa, Kamal, Stoneham and the other two men all received the same rough handling, each being pushed, unceremoniously, into their respective vehicles. The shocked and frightened crowds outside watched as the convoy pulled away from The Blue Mosque.

Six police cars, sirens and horns blaring, wove their way through the busy old-city traffic. As Jack was thrown about in the back seat, he saw one of the cars in front turn off from the convoy and head up a small side street. The blaring horns continued, the police drivers, oblivious to the danger they were putting other vehicles and pedestrians in, continued to scream through the narrow streets.

Miraculously without incident, they arrived at the central police station. Ten or twelve other officers waited eagerly outside, obviously keen to be involved, in some small way, in the capture of the band of terrorists. The cars all lined up and the suspects were roughly dragged into the building. There was pandemonium inside as Jack and the rest were brought to the main processing area. General Kamal caught Jack's eye and winked, Jack nodded and gave the slightest of smiles. An officer noticed Jack's grin and punched him hard in the stomach.

'Hey, leave him alone,' shouted Lisa.

Jack recovered and straightened up. Through winded breath, he said, 'I'm okay.'

A couple of female officer took hold of Lisa and, as she was hauled-off to the women's area, shouted to Jack, 'Where the hell is Stoneham?'

It was late afternoon when Jack, Lisa, General Kamal and his men, were herded into the large briefing room of Istanbul's Central Police Station. Two senior police officers, along with Istanbul's Chief of Police were seated across from the group of foreigners, their faces clearly showing the anger they felt at the unexpected turn of events.

The room was filled to capacity with the arrival of the American Deputy Ambassador, the British Chief of Mission and the Saudi Arabian Ambassador, along with several aides and attaches.

Documents were produced to verify the suspects were actually in the process of capturing an international terrorist and that, once formalities had been completed, the suspects must be released to their respective Embassies. The Turkish Chief of Police was even more angry and embarrassed, when it was stated the actual terrorist, Gregory Stoneham, had managed to escape while in police custody.

Chapter Fifty Eight
'The Saudi Embassy'

The Saudi Ambassador stood in front of his desk. 'His Majesty sends his compliments, Mr Castle, and also to you, General Kamal. I am to extend any and all support. So if there is anything you require, please let me know.'

'Thank you, sir,' said Jack.

Kamal went over and spoke quietly to the Ambassador and, after bidding them and Lisa, 'Good evening,' the Ambassador left the room.

The three sat down. For several seconds nothing was said, then Lisa spoke, 'What the hell happened today?'

'Yes, General,' said Jack, 'how did you manage to show up in the right place, at the right time?'

Kamal smiled, 'I am head of Saudi intelligence, my dear. And I'm sure you didn't mind me and my men, showing-up, as you put it? All things considered.'

'Oh, we're pleased you did,' said Lisa, 'but how did you know?'

'That does not matter for the moment, my dear.'

Jack looked at Lisa. 'Who was the shooter? Was he the intermediary you met last night?'

Lisa shook her head, 'No. He was nothing like the guy in the club.'

Kamal stood up and took a folder from the Ambassador's desk, then returned to his seat. 'His name was Marco Vilnus, a Russian national. His passport showed he'd recently been in America and returned to Russia by way of Canada. Arrived in Istanbul yesterday morning.'

Jack leaned back into the gold-silk couch. 'We've not asked the most important question. What happened to Stoneham? He got away. We failed.'

Kamal stood up. 'Failed? You haven't failed, my dear. The mission was to secure the antidote and stop thousands of people from dying. And that's exactly what you did.'

That's right,' said Lisa. 'If you hadn't saved Hana Chang's life, we'd not have been able to trade her for the formulae.'

Jack shook his head. 'But we still lost Stoneham.'

'I think you're being a little hard on yourself, my dear. You captured him. It was the Turks who lost him.'

Lisa leaned forward. 'How the hell did he manage to escape anyway? He must have had contacts in the Turkish police?'

Kamal picked up the folder again. 'No, my dear. He killed the two officers, that's how he escaped.'

'How?' said Lisa.

The general flipped another page. 'The initial report suggests the officers were killed with a long stiletto blade or slim short sword.'

'The walking cane!'

Kamal and Lisa looked at Jack.

'His walking cane,' said Jack, again. 'The bloody stick had a weapon in it.'

Chapter Fifty Nine
'Mr Washington'

The big office in the First Merchant Bank of Montenegro smelled heavily of cigar smoke. The fat banker held open a large mahogany humidor. 'Please try one of these. The ones on the left are Cuban, on the right, Bolivian. The Cuban's are particularly good.' He looked at his computer and continued. 'Now let me see. You asked for a final balance to include all funds, minus charges and transfer fees.'

Several seconds passed as his client carefully snipped-off the end of his cigar and lit-up.

'Yes, sir. Here we are,' said the banker. 'Seven million, five-hundred and forty thousand, dollars.'

The other man nodded and exhaled a plume of blue-grey smoke. 'Hmm these are excellent,' he said, as rolled the cigar between his fingers. 'Okay. Transfer the seven million, hold onto the half million, and I'll take the forty thousand in cash today.'

The fat man smiled. 'And the transfer goes to?'

The man slipped a small card across the desk. The banker picked it up and read aloud, 'Banco Centrale de Philippines. Very good, sir.'

Several more minutes passed as the transaction was completed.

There was a knock at the door. 'Come in,' said the banker.

A young man entered carrying a small attaché case. He placed it on the desk and left. The man unclipped the locks and flicked through the bundles of hundred dollar bills.

The banker smiled. 'It's all there, sir,'

The man closed the case and stood up. 'I'm sure it is.' He held out his hand. 'Thank you for all your help. I'll be in touch very soon.'

The fat banker shook hands, a large smile on his sweaty face. 'Thank you, Mr Washington.'

Chapter Sixty
'Danny Boy'

The rain had stopped as the coffin was carried from the tiny church in Dunmuiry, on the outskirts of Belfast. The wind, particularly cold for late summer, blew across from the Irish Sea, and chilled the fifty or so mourners, as they followed the pall-bearers into the pretty cemetery.

Lisa's arm was hooked through Jack's as they, and Mathew, walked behind Ryan's family and close friends. At the graveside the cortege came to a stop. Six big men reverently lowered the coffin onto the supports above the open grave, and stepped back. The old vicar cleared his throat and began the eulogy, while a young girl played *Danny Boy,* on a penny whistle.

'I never got a chance to know anything about him,' whispered Lisa.

'Me neither,' whispered Jack. 'He was a charmer though.'

Through her tears, Lisa agreed. 'He was indeed.'

Epilogue

After capturing Hana Chang, and given her status as a Colonel in the North Korean Secret Service, the Saudi Arabian Government declared her actions as an act of war on behalf of one sovereign nation against another. The Americans and Brits were quick to jump on the bandwagon, with both governments supporting the Saudi's position. The North Koreans however quickly diffused the escalating crisis by publically and categorically declaring General Chang, and his subordinate, Colonel Hana Chang were acting alone in recruiting the ex-CIA agent, Gregory Stoneham and undertaking the attack on the said nations.

Following the contamination of Blackton Reservoir, the final death toll in the North East of England was over thirteen hundred, men, women and children. That number would have risen to the unthinkable, without the securing of the Baghdad virus antidote. Thanks to the swift actions of the security services and the military cordon, the virus was contained, but there were still over six-hundred of the local populous arrested and charged with various offences from public disorder to riot and looting.

The death toll in Washington DC, following the contamination of the McMillan Reservoir, was greater than the UK, at almost two-thousand citizens. Four of the souls that perished were Mr Henry Madsen, Mrs Connie Madsen, their son Davy Madsen and their little daughter, Lucy.

Seventy-two hours after the explosion in the Zamzam storage facility, Colonel Hana Chang was flown to Hong Kong. Dressed in denims jeans, a white T-shirt and white Nikes' she was escorted by four Saudi security officers to the British Embassy. Waiting for her were Porton Down's top microbiologist, Professor Andrew McClean and her father, General Chang. After Professor McClean confirmed the viability of the Baghdad Virus formulae, Hana Chang and her father were free to go.

Three days after Lisa Reynard left North Korea, Colonel Hana Chang's naked body was found in her Pyongyang apartment. The post-mortem report said she had died from a massive coronary embolism. What the report did not say, nor did it speculate on, was why, and how, could such a fit and healthy woman as Colonel Chang, ever succumb to a heart attack.

For failing in the planned Baghdad virus mission, and then supplying secret information to MI6, General Chang was tried and convicted of treason. His trial took twenty-five minutes, after which he was executed by a six-man firing squad, in the courtyard of Nandook Prison. His family were billed for the cost of the cremation. A second bill was received for the cost of the six bullets.

Al Bilad, the national newspaper of Saudi Arabia, ran a headline editorial on the attack in Mecca. *The attempt by international terrorists to wreak havoc on this year's Hajj did not go as these vile individuals planned. Two devices exploded in the facilities area of the Al-Haram Mosque, resulting in the death of one young Asian national, Mr Naga Pradeshi.*

Major Ibrahim Masood, a respected Saudi officer, thwarted the other terrorists atrocity and prevented many more deaths. Sadly Major Masood died in the second blast.

Bosnian State Security submitted an extradition order from the United States, for Dushan Grasic. The Americans quickly and happily agreed to the extradition and will be handing him over as soon as he has served thirty five years in prison, for his part in the murder of a Miami Police Officer.

In Mogadishu, the little Indian watched as Commander Aidid held the stone up to the light.

'Tell me again,' said the commander, a huge smile on his shiny black face.

The Indian pushed out his bony chest and said with pride, 'In order to yield the greatest possible residual weight, the stone has been emerald-cut. You now hold a Kashmiri sapphire with a current value of two-hundred and fifteen thousand dollars.'

The diplomatic registration plate denoted the Bentley had come from the Saudi Arabian Embassy. Jack watched as the elegant vehicle came to an almost silent stop in front of the house. The chauffeur opened the door and a young attaché stepped out. 'Mr Castle, sir?'

'Yes, I'm Jack Castle.'

'Good morning, sir.' He handed Jack a large embossed envelope, and said, 'With His Majesty's compliments, sir.'

Inside was a hand written letter from the ruler of the Kingdom of Saudi Arabia . . .

My Dear Jack.

On Behalf of myself and my people, we would like to thank you for your resourcefulness, courage and support, in protecting our nation from what could have been a most devastating terrorist attack. We sincerely hope you are well recovered from your injuries and, when you feel fully recuperated, we would like to offer our thanks in person. We would therefore be honoured if you and your family would join us in our home in Riyadh, at your convenience.

With our deepest thanks and God's holy blessing.

R . . .

.

Printed in Great Britain
by Amazon